Beauty
and the
BEAST

A LATTER-DAY TALE

Beauty *and the* BEAST

A LATTER-DAY TALE

A Novel by
Jennifer Jan Brough

Based on the screenplay by
Brittany Wiscombe

Dedicated to the memory of
Rulon and Margaret Brough

This novel is a work of fiction, based on the original 1756 story by Madame Le Prince de Beaumont. Any resemblance to actual persons, living or dead, is entirely coincidental and should be construed as such.

www.CandlelightMedia.com

ISBN-10
0-9709151-7-9

ISBN-13
978-0-97091-517-9

Printed in the United States of America

Chapter One

Once upon a time, in a land not unlike your own, there lived a man named Eric Landry. He was in his 30s, extremely good-looking and managed to keep a year-round tan. He lived in utter luxury, in a great mansion with far more rooms than a single businessman who traveled could ever need, let alone use.

He wore only the best clothes and drove the finest of automobiles. But no one envied him for his wealth. He was a cold-hearted man who lived almost completely alone, with only a housekeeper and his money for company. He kept to himself, thereby preventing anyone from really knowing anything about him. And so the rumors started.

Due to his treatment of the few unfortunate souls who did come in contact with him, Eric became known to the townspeople as the Beast. He wasn't always this way, but what mattered was the present. And so most people who needed to come to Landry Mansion quickly completed their business so they didn't have to face Eric any longer than necessary.

Eric sat at the breakfast table, sneering at his plate of food. He was difficult to please and even harder to live with. Mrs. Haygood, a kindly widow in her 50s, was his housekeeper. Having raised three children, she was used to tantrums and had the learned patience of an experienced mother. She knew when to push Eric and when to stay out of his way. She didn't let his moods bring her down.

That didn't stop Eric from trying.

"Mrs. Haygood!" Eric bellowed, scowling at the steaming French toast. It was dusted with powdered sugar. He noticed the raspberry sauce that dripped down the side of the toast, and the scowl deepened.

"Yes, Eric?" Mrs. Haygood replied calmly as she entered the kitchen.

"What's this?" he asked, indicating the fluffy meal with disgust.

"Breakfast."

"No, it's not." He pushed the plate away and stood up to leave. "When you find anything for me to eat, bring it to my office."

He grumbled to himself and left in his predictably gruff manner. Mrs. Haygood smiled and shook her head.

"I guess I'll just toast a bagel then."

She looked at the beautiful breakfast that Eric had so rudely dismissed and with a sigh scooped it into the garbage. If he didn't like the food when it was fresh, two-day-old leftovers in the fridge would make his mood even worse. A shame really, because he loved this breakfast last week.

Eric stormed off toward his in-home office. His work as a freelance consultant took him all over the country, so when he wasn't traveling, he preferred to work out of his enormous home. This morning his mood was worse than usual. He passed his front entryway and paid no attention to the smartly-dressed woman who came through the door.

Vanessa, Eric's assistant, tugged at her suit jacket, making sure everything was in its proper place. She adjusted her grip on the briefcase she held in one hand, and grabbed a file from it with the other.

"Eric," she called after him, "I have the Snyder file done, and I got a call from the Jensen Corporation."

This caught enough of his attention so that Eric paused his trek to his office. He turned to face his assistant, a look of thin tolerance on his face. For her part, Vanessa didn't miss a beat.

"They want to set up a meeting, and have you fly out to consult for a week," she continued.

"Let me clap for joy later." The annoyance in Eric's tone was hard to miss.

He turned to resume his journey to his office and commanded, "Bring me the file, and then I have some emails I need you to follow up on."

Vanessa rolled her eyes and sighed at his back.

"You're welcome," she muttered. Vanessa worked hard. She tried to tolerate Eric's many moods and demands. But a person could only take so much abuse for so long and she had about reached that point. She sighed again and then steeled herself for another day of work with the Beast.

Vanessa got to the office and took the file of emails Eric handed her and gave him the Snyder file. There was no speaking, and truth be told, Vanessa preferred it that way. If there was no talking, there was less chance of facing Eric's wrath. Eric rose from his desk a few minutes later and exited the office. Vanessa immediately relaxed, her normal reaction when he wasn't around.

Eric stormed down the main hallway, his footsteps echoing on the hardwood floor. Mrs. Haygood heard the rumble from the kitchen. She could determine his mood by the volume of his footsteps. *Sounds like a winner of a mood today*, she thought. She called out to him as he passed through the kitchen.

"Oh, Eric. The repairman is coming by this afternoon to fix the fireplace." Eric's pace faltered a moment.

"Do I care?" he snapped.

"It's just a reminder," Mrs. Haygood said cheerfully. She was always cheerful and that got on Eric's nerves, making his bad mood worse.

"Mrs. Haygood, when have I ever listened to your mundane reminders?" He paused to glare at her, condescension oozing out of every pore. "Do they really serve any purpose?"

Mrs. Haygood kept her smile firmly in place. She had learned long ago not to let his tone get to her. She adopted her motherly pose, complete with her hands on her hips.

"Just keeping you informed so you don't blame me later for not telling you."

"When has that ever happened?" Eric asked, what little patience he had rapidly evaporating.

She smiled, her point made and then replied, "Two weeks ago, when you screamed at the electrician for interrupting your 'need' for solitude."

He didn't reply. Instead, blood boiled back to the surface of his skin, and Eric stalked off.

Mrs. Haygood sighed to the empty room. "You live alone, Eric. Why do you need solitude anyway?"

Sometimes she just did not understand him. After all the years she had lived in his house and worked for him, she knew Eric pretty well, probably better than anyone. But still moments like these made her wonder if she really knew him at all.

Elsewhere in the land, there lived a twenty-something young woman named Belle Watson. More than anything Belle loved her family. She had her father, two brothers and one sister. Her mother died unexpectedly years ago. Belle worked hard as an orthodontic assistant and had gone back to school in pursuit of a Masters degree. Everything Belle did was with her family in mind. Throughout the town she was known as a kind person, someone who reached out to help others and who quickly brought a smile to the faces of all she met.

Belle looked up from the computer to check the time on the wall clock. *Closing time.* She clicked on the button that would begin the shut down procedure for the front desk computer. The orthodontist had left earlier, but Belle and Anna, her friend who also worked at the office, stayed to update files, make appointment reminder calls, and make sure things were prepared for the next day.

Anna came through the treatment area, shutting off lights as she went. Her purse was slung over her shoulder and her coat was in hand. It had been a long day and both were eager to go home.

"Ready?" Anna asked, straightening her pretty blonde pony tail in the mirror.

"Almost. Let me water the plants. You go ahead—I'll lock up," Belle said, reaching under the sink for the watering can.

"Want me to do it?" Anna asked. "You have your *homework.*"

"This will only take a minute, and I totally hear your tone there, Anna."

"What?" Anna replied with mock innocence. She grinned.

"Don't knock the homework thing."

Belle filled the watering can and took it to each of the plants around the office.

"I have complete respect for it," Anna said, watching her friend work. "I've been there. You have too. For some reason, you're still going. What are you going to do with an MBA anyway?"

"Probably buy this practice and fire you for mocking me," Belle teased back.

"Fine," Anna said with a laugh. "Are we still on for tomorrow?"

"Yeah, with your cousin."

"Do you like him?" Anna asked.

"Craig? He seems . . . nice," Belle replied hesitantly.

"He's not bad-looking."

"No, it's not that. I . . . I really don't know him yet," she explained, reaching for the right words.

"Well, you can get to know him better tomorrow," Anna replied, pulling her coat on over her scrubs. She started digging through her purse for her keys.

"All right. See you later," Belle said.

Anna frowned until she held up her keys triumphantly. She grinned and headed out the door.

"Later!"

Belle watered the remaining plants, then grabbed her purse, locked the door and left.

Belle's father, Walter Watson, worked as a repairman. He'd always been good with his hands and had recently found employment doing repair work for the people in town. He enjoyed the tasks he was assigned and always looked forward to what new challenges the day would bring. That is, until the day his boss handed him a particular work order. 'Fireplace repair at the Landry Mansion,' it said. Watson had never met Mr. Landry, but he had heard the talk around town. He'd never been one to listen to rumors, though, so he decided he wouldn't start now.

Watson knelt down in front of the fireplace. The brick dug into his knees as he leaned forward to get a look inside the chimney of the fireplace. He shined his flashlight and checked the flue. He spied the problem and reached for his tools.

Watson was working diligently when he heard voices coming down the hall. One had to be Mr. Landry. He thought the lighter, feminine voice might be Mr. Landry's assistant, but wasn't sure. He continued working as the volume of the conversation increased.

"You're the most incompetent assistant ever!" Eric shouted. "I told you not to call until I approved."

"But you did!" Vanessa protested.

"I told you specifically not to do a thing until we had them locked in. This will end my relationship with them!" Eric bellowed angrily.

"Like you have a relationship with anyone, working or otherwise," Vanessa muttered to herself. She froze as she saw Eric go rigid.

"You're fired," Eric said firmly.

Vanessa was incensed. She gathered her wits enough to reach into her briefcase and pull out a piece of paper.

"Don't bother. I've had my resignation typed for weeks." She handed Eric the paper.

Watson had stopped working as the argument escalated. He watched the confrontation until Eric's eyes suddenly shifted in his direction. Watson's heart skipped a beat at being caught. Quickly he turned back to his work. Eric looked at the letter in his hands.

"Judging by the date on this then, I don't have to pay you for the last few weeks of your laziness," he retaliated.

Fuming, Vanessa tore the paper out of his hand and stormed out the front door, slamming it as she went. Watson quickly finished the repair and gathered his tools. He continued to think about the argument he had witnessed.

He was so lost in thought that he wasn't paying attention to where he was going. Watson bumped into an antique urn which sat on a pillar near the fireplace. It wobbled a second and then crashed to the ground, splintering into several pieces on the hard flooring. Watson gasped in shock.

"Idiot!" Eric yelled, racing towards the bumbling repairman.

Watson tried to pick up the pieces, but was so nervous he kept dropping them.

"I'm so sorry, sir! I didn't mean to—" he tried to apologize.

"Didn't mean to? No one tries to be an idiot, it always just happens!" Eric shouted.

Eric tore the urn piece from Watson's hands and looked at it with obvious distress.

"Do you have any idea how much this was worth? This is worth the lives of ten people, twenty if they're you!"

Watson felt awful. His heart was pounding and the adrenaline rush was hitting him.

"I'm terribly sorry, Mr. Landry," he stammered. "What can I do to make it up to you?"

"You couldn't possibly do enough," Eric scoffed. He checked his watch. "I'm calling your boss first thing in the morning. Start looking for a new job."

Watson's eyes widened in horror. He couldn't lose his job. He had his family to think about.

"No, sir, please, I need—" he pleaded.

"I don't care what you need. This is broken, my day is spoiled, and you're to blame for both!"

Watson knew there was no reasoning with Eric at this point. But he couldn't give up.

"Please, Mr. Landry, I can't be fired; my children depend on me, and I can't—"

"Get out now, before I call the police!" Eric demanded.

Would he really? Watson thought. He quickly gathered his tools and left with head bowed and shoulders drooping. Eric watched the man go and then went briskly back to his office.

Watson drove slowly home. He worried over what to do. How could he tell his family? Belle worked so hard to help, rarely thinking of her own needs and wishes. His son, James, was serving a mission in Belgium. James needed to focus on the work he was doing, and not worry about his family's financial difficulties. And his two younger children, Mike and Kelli, they just needed to enjoy being kids. They already had been through more than any child should when they lost their mother. Still having no solution, Watson did the only thing he knew he could do. He began to pray.

Watson put on a brave face when he came home. He didn't want anyone to know anything was wrong just yet. Belle was preparing dinner while Kelli, his teenage daughter, was chatting nonstop as she set the table.

"I got a 79 on my math test but Ms. Parker says she'll curve the test anyway," Kelli said, pushing her long reddish brown hair out of her way.

"You're lucky she curves the scores," Belle replied, stirring dinner in the skillet. A quick taste told her it was done and she dumped it into a serving dish.

"Yeah, I know!" Kelli said.

"Yeah, I know!" Mike repeated. Though twelve years old, he was still at the stage of being an annoying pest to his older siblings. Kelli stuck out her tongue at him.

"Mike, stop acting like a 7-year-old," Kelli said, clearly annoyed.

"Mike, stop acting like a—" he began to parrot back and then stopped when he realized what she had said.

Belle tried to get Kelli back on track.

"Kelli, why not try to do better, so you don't have to rely on a curve?"

Kelli appeared to consider the suggestion for a minute and then shrugged it off.

"Guess what I learned in seminary today?"

Belle glanced into the living room where her father sat. He looked rather glum in his favorite chair. Mike and Kelli pulled her attention back to them before she could give her father any more thought.

"Mike, put this on the table," Belle said. She passed him a dish. "What, Kelli?"

"Well, we were talking about life after death, and how we're all judged and all that. And then someone said they heard that animals will have a say at the judgment bar," Kelli explained.

"Okay . . . what, so like pets?" Belle asked.

"I guess. Brenda said she's probably going to be kicked out of heaven if her dog says anything. She never walked him and always pushed him off her bed."

Belle laughed. "I think Brenda will find the judgment bar isn't only about what her old dog says."

After placing a pitcher of water on the center of the table, Belle glanced at her father.

"Dad, we're ready."

He slowly got up and joined the family at the table. Belle noticed his unsteady movements and was sure something was up.

"Probably," Kelli said, still thinking about seminary. "Brenda lies all the time so I'm sure she's not going to make it to heaven anyway."

"Kelli!" Belle shook her head.

Mike giggled. Everyone sat down at the table.

"What are we talking about?" Watson asked his family.

"Well . . . " Belle started but was interrupted by Mike.

"We're all going to be judged by animals at a bar," Mike reported matter-of-factly.

Everyone was stunned into silence until Kelli started to laugh. Before things got any more out of hand, Belle quickly folded her arms.

"Who's blessing the food?" she asked.

After dinner, Mike quickly stood up. "Can I play a video game?"

"Not now, Mike. Why don't you help Kelli clean up the kitchen?" Belle suggested.

Mike groaned. "Okay."

The two younger kids gathered the dirty dishes and the leftover food. Watson had long since left the table and returned to his chair in the living room. Belle left the kids to it and went to talk to her father.

"Dad?" She couldn't hide the concern in her voice.

Watson tried to sit straighter in his chair and give the appearance that all was well.

"Yeah?"

Belle sat across from him on the sofa.

"What's wrong? You've been quiet all evening."

He tried to smile reassuringly, but then gave up and let the smile break into a frown.

"I need to start looking for a new job," he replied.

Belle was shocked. She looked in the direction of the kitchen and saw the kids playing with the dish soap, thankfully oblivious to the conversation in the living room.

"Why? What happened?" Belle asked.

"It was an accident," he began, shaking his head. "I broke some art piece at Mr. Landry's, and he said he'll call my boss in the morning. I'll be fired."

"Dad, did you try to talk him out of it?"

"Of course I did, but the man is a . . . a beast!" Watson

said, raising his voice. "He even threatened to call the police on me!"

"For what? It was an accident." The gall of Mr. Landry!

Watson leaned forward, his head hanging down and eyes downcast. He had begun wringing his hands as the tale unfolded.

"Dad?"

"It doesn't change anything. I've only had the job for a few months. Mr. Landry is a powerful man, and a spiteful one. Everyone knows it, at church, in town, everyone!" The desperation rang clearly in his voice.

Belle paused to think. *He's right. But there has to be a way to fix this. Maybe I can reason with this Mr. Landry.* She made a decision. She would go and see Mr. Landry, speak with him, and make him see reason.

"Let me see what I can do," she said, breaking the relative silence. Mike and Kelli were finished cleaning the kitchen, and now blew soap bubbles at each other.

"No Belle, this is my problem," her dad tried to object.

"Dad, we all need you to keep this job. If I can do something to help, I'm doing it."

As she drove up to the Landry Mansion, Belle found herself wondering if this was as great an idea as she had thought it was back in the safety of her living room. The mansion seemed ominous and foreboding to Belle. She took in the whole of the enormous house as she gathered her courage at the end of the long driveway. She had not gone very far up its length when she came upon a wrought iron fence, its spikes adding to the 'keep out' feeling of the whole property. Belle pulled up to the intercom box. Taking a deep breath to gather her courage, she pressed the buzzer.

"Yes?" a pleasant female voice answered.

"Is Eric Landry available?" Belle asked. She half-expected a gruff man to answer.

"Your name?"

"Belle Watson. He doesn't know me," Belle replied.

"What is this regarding?" the voice asked.

"My father, uh, from the repair company today . . . ?"

There was a pause and then the voice continued.

"Drive on in. He's on the grounds at the back of the property. Just walk around the back of the estate, and you'll find Mr. Landry."

"Thank you." The gate opened. It seemed to settle with a thud. Taking a breath, Belle drove on through and headed up to the mansion. She parked in front of the imposing estate and paused to gather her thoughts.

Belle made a closer inspection of the house and noticed how well manicured the grounds were. She hated to walk on the trimmed grass, even if it was browning now with the winter cold. But the lady on the intercom had said to walk behind the estate. There wasn't much light so she walked slowly.

She rounded the corner and found herself in a tree-lined tunnel. *This must be absolutely beautiful in the sunlight*, she thought. A light breeze was blowing and the trees seemed to come alive, groaning and rustling. She stopped suddenly and looked around. Belle felt as though she was not alone.

"Hello?" Belle called out. The only response was a rustling sound behind her. Slowly she turned.

She gasped.

Before her stood a dark figure. Belle took a step back and the figure moved forward. A sliver of moonlight shown across him, illuminating part of his face. It was more handsome than she thought it would be, based on all the stories about his temper.

"What are you doing on my property?" he demanded in a low voice that seemed tight, like he would snap any second.

She swallowed nervously, still a little shaken from his sudden appearance.

"Are you Mr. Landry?" she managed to ask.

The man didn't answer in words. He stood there glaring at her for what felt like forever. It was clear this was Eric Landry. Before she could speak again, he grabbed her arm and led her roughly to the patio before releasing her. Belle tried to maintain a calm demeanor as she straightened her coat and scarf. Feeling back together, she looked at Mr. Landry defiantly. There was more light here, and she could see he stood with his legs planted firmly, his grey suit pants peaking out from under a long, black dress coat. He was an imposing figure, to say the least.

"I've come to ask you not to call my father's boss," she stated bravely. He frowned.

"You're the repairman's daughter?"

She nodded.

"You must be an idiot as well."

Belle balked at his words.

"Excuse me, but that's uncalled for—as is the way you treated my father." All her earlier trepidation evaporated.

"Treated him? You want me to reward him for breaking priceless art?"

"No, of course not," Belle said, struggling to be polite. "But don't call his boss. We need him to work. My family relies on him."

"Do you know what fine art costs?" he asked.

"Everything here is expensive—how could he avoid it?" she replied indignantly.

Eric reached out with a black leather gloved hand and grabbed her by the elbow. He'd had it with her intrusion on his privacy.

"You're trespassing. Get out."

Belle pulled back.

"No, no, wait!"

She must have sounded desperate enough because he stopped.

"I didn't come here to upset you," she tried to smooth things over. "Please, I have a younger sister and two brothers, one of whom is on a mission, and we need to support them all."

"Have your mother start working then."

She winced at the mention of her mother.

"My mother died years ago. I help as much as I can, but my father's job is what we rely on."

"Lovely sob story, but it doesn't change anything. I was wronged—"

"It was an accident," Belle interrupted him, "and if you want it made up to you, well, I'm sorry. We can't pay you anything close to what the art is probably worth. But firing my father won't help."

"It'll make me feel better," he challenged angrily.

Belle glared at him.

"Will it?" She looked away, calming herself down with a deep breath. "Please, there must be something I can do, some way we can make it right."

Eric looked at her intensely, trying to determine if she was worth the effort.

"All right," he conceded. "I just fired my assistant today. You'll replace her."

Belle was shocked. But before she could say anything, he went on.

"You'll work for me until I feel the debt is paid off."

Belle found her voice. "But I have a job."

"Should I call your dad's boss?" he threatened.

Belle shook her head.

"What do you do?" he asked.

"I'm a part-time assistant at an orthodontics office."

Eric huffed at that.

"You're working part-time but you claim your family's desperate?" he pointed out.

"I work part-time and also go to school," she explained.

"You have your work cut out for you then. Whenever you're not working, you come here. You start tomorrow."

He crossed over the patio and went to one of the back doors. He paused at the door and turned back.

"Go out the way you came in."

She stood there a moment more, not quite able to believe what had just happened. She heard the sound of the door opening.

"Thank you, Mr. Landry," she called out meekly.

He made no indication that he had heard her thanks. She stood there frozen until the slam of the door behind him startled her out of her stupor. She shook her head and began to make her way back through the tree-lined tunnel. As she drove home, Belle felt relieved that the confrontation was over and a little nervous about what was to come. She would be working at Landry Mansion on an almost daily basis. She'd heard the rumors and the gossip in town, but never participated in it. Now she was beginning to wonder if she should have listened more carefully.

Watson sat still in his favorite chair, staring at a picture of his late wife. His eyes were wet with unshed tears. At the sound of the front door opening, he quickly wiped his eyes and put on his best brave face.

"Dad?" Belle called out.

Watson stood from his chair as Belle walked in.

"What happened?" he asked.

Belle sat on the couch.

"I spoke to him. Everything will be all right." She sighed and took off her coat and gloves.

"But how?" Watson asked, stunned.

"I'm going to work for him for awhile," Belle said. She tried to smile.

Her father was beyond concerned.

"With that man?" he said, rising from his seat. "What about your job? And your classes?"

"I'll manage," she said, trying to reassure her father. "It's only until he feels the debt has been paid, and at least you'll keep your job."

"Oh Belle!" Watson shook his head. "No, this is too much."

"Dad, it's the only way." She smiled reassuringly. "It'll be all right."

Belle rose from her seat, kissed her dad on the forehead and went to her room.

Chapter Two

*H*er first day working for Eric Landry did not start well. Belle had been focused on her work at the orthodontics office and then noticed the time. She scrambled to finish her work before the next assistant came in for the rest of the day. She moved around the office in a whirl of activity, updating files of patients treated that day and putting things back where they belonged. With purse and coat in hand, Belle was almost ready to go.

Anna met her at the door, ready to leave as well.

"Craig should be here soon," Anna said excitedly.

"What?"

"For the exhibit. Today, remember?" Anna reminded her.

"Oh, I can't go." Belle fished her keys out of her purse.

"Why not?"

"Long story," Belle said, shaking her head.

"But Craig's been asking about you since you guys met. He had me set this up just so you'd come."

"I'm sorry, Anna. I just can't go."

"Is it something about him you don't like?"

Belle laughed. "No, no. I just have another . . . commitment."

"Really?" Anna asked suspiciously. There had been far more inventive excuses made to get out of a date.

Belle was anxious to get on her way. She didn't want to

risk annoying Mr. Landry. But Anna was a good friend. Frustrated, she tried again to explain.

"Anna, I'm not trying to blow him off . . . "

Before she could finish Craig walked in. His average looks and the confidence he projected as he moved caught Belle's attention. But she had other more important things to worry about.

"Hey!" Craig said excitedly.

Belle took a deep breath and walked past him. She turned back apologetically.

"Hi Craig. Sorry, I've got to go," she said, and with that, she left.

Craig looked back at Anna for an explanation.

"Uh, she's going to have to go with us another day," Anna said.

"Why?" he asked. He couldn't hide the disappointment in his voice.

"She didn't say."

Craig sighed and shoved his hands in his pockets. Anna smiled, looped her hand through his arm and pulled him with her.

"Is it something I said?" he asked. Anna tried to hold back a laugh and shook her head.

Belle drove home as quickly as she safely could. She'd gone through her closet the night before and pulled out her most business-like outfit. Working for Dr. Thompson at the orthodontics office didn't require suits or fancy executive-style blouses. Everyone wore scrubs. And with money tight because of school expenses, Belle didn't waste anything on clothes she wouldn't need. Now, she would have to do the best she could with what she had and hope that Mr. Landry would let it go.

She changed into her dress slacks and a crisp button-up shirt. She finished it off with a simple jacket and was out the door.

Belle stood at the front door of the mansion and straightened her jacket. She checked her hair in the reflection of a glass window. Then with a deep breath, she rang the bell. She stood there for several minutes until she heard footsteps coming her way. She braced herself for Mr. Landry and was surprised to see a kind, older woman open the door. Belle figured she must be the person with whom she spoke over the intercom.

"You must be the new assistant," the lady said with a smile. "I'm Mrs. Haygood, the housekeeper. Come on in." She motioned Belle inside as she stepped back, opening the door wider. Belle hesitantly entered the house.

"Eric is expecting you," Mrs. Haygood said. "Follow me." Belle nodded.

As she followed Mrs. Haygood, Belle glanced around to acquaint herself with the new surroundings. The house was richly decorated. Plush couches, precious art pieces, and glittering fixtures were everywhere. She couldn't help but feel awed as she looked around. Mrs. Haygood was talking so she forced herself to pay attention.

" . . . Now don't let him frighten you. And when you're hungry, just come see me in the kitchen. I'll fix you something delicious." Mrs. Haygood smiled reassuringly.

"Thank you."

They stopped in front of an imposing wooden door. *This must be his office,* Belle thought. The housekeeper indicated she should go on in and so, gathering her courage, Belle pushed opened the door and walked in to see Eric engrossed in papers and a laptop.

He didn't react at all to her entrance. Maybe he didn't even know she was there. Belle debated about clearing her throat or saying something—

"You should knock," he said suddenly. Belle almost jumped.

Unsure of what to do, she started to turn back to the door to try again when his voice stopped her.

"Shut the door," he commanded.

She shut the door and noticed that Mrs. Haygood was gone. She had never felt so alone in her life. She offered a silent prayer as she stood in the middle of the room. The awkwardness made her feel unsure of what to do next. Belle didn't dare ask because she was afraid of setting off Mr. Landry.

As for him, Eric continued to focus on his work. He quickly signed a document and then dropped his pen heavily, startling Belle yet again. He looked at her for a long moment, leaning back in his chair. He seemed to be studying her, making some kind of judgment. Finally he spoke.

"Do you have a name?" he asked apathetically.

"Belle."

His lips curled upward in a sneering grin. "Good. When I ring, you come."

Belle blinked. His humor was also part of his meanness, she decided.

"Uh, no. Not the kind you ring. It means 'beauty.'"

He looked her up and down. "If you say so."

His words hit her like a physical blow. Before she could think of some way to counter him politely, he pushed his chair back from his desk and stood. Eric indicated she should follow and then led her through his office to a small desk in a little room off to the side.

"You'll work here, when you're not running errands," he explained.

Belle frowned. "Errands?" she asked.

Eric raised an eyebrow at her questioning him. Then he reached into his pocket and pulled out a piece of paper. She gulped as she took it from his outstretched hand and began to read down the long list of tasks. *Oh, he is enjoying this entirely too much.*

Without another word, Eric turned and went back to his office. Belle sighed. *Better get to work. The sooner I start, the sooner this nightmare is over,* she thought to herself.

Three hours later, Belle struggled to get the door open. She had several freshly dry-cleaned suits and shirts in one hand. In the other was a stack of copied documents. It was difficult, but she managed to balance it all and still move forward to Eric's office. She found him on the phone.

"Yes. Well, your mid-level managers are abysmal," he said with no emotion.

Belle stumbled through the door with her arms full. Eric glared at her, annoyed at the interruption. Belle tried to gently set down the copied documents.

They slid off the desk and scattered on the floor.

Covering the receiver with one hand, Eric fixed her with a cold glare and said, "Do you mind?"

Belle thought about telling him that she did mind, and he could certainly help her—but she quickly discarded that thought.

"Put the documents there," he indicated a nearby table, "and the suits go in my closet."

His commands issued, Eric returned to his phone call. Belle could have sworn he smiled with pleasure as he watched her struggle to collect the documents and not drop the suits.

"Don, I'll be honest with you," Eric said, focusing back on his conversation, "you either need to train them quickly or rethink your quarterly earnings projections."

Belle left the office. She closed the door behind her and sighed in relief just to be out of his hostile presence. She readjusted her grip on the suits and started down the hallway through the mansion.

As she wandered through the large rooms, she took a closer look at Eric's home. The dining room was elegant with fine china and crystal in a hutch that looked as though it was rarely used. She passed several bedrooms with decor she had never seen before except in magazines. She checked a few of the closets but none seemed used. *Not Eric's room*, she figured.

A glare of sunlight caught her eye and she peeked into what appeared to be an exercise room. A punching bag hung in one corner, and various pieces of fitness equipment were spread about the other side of the room. Open space was left in the center and a mirror lined one wall. Another wall sported hooks with martial arts equipment and gear. She continued on her quest, passing a sunlit spa room with a large Jacuzzi, and just on the other side was an elaborate swimming pool. She passed even more bedrooms and couldn't help but be awed by the rich luxury Eric lived in.

Belle realized she didn't know which room was Eric's. A master bedroom for Mr. Landry would be large and masculine, she guessed. She came to a double-doored room and figured that had to be it. But instead she found a beautiful sitting room, complete with a fireplace. Bookshelves surrounded a little nook by the fireplace. Belle put the suits down on a nearby chair and went to explore Landry's reading collection. She scanned the shelf and was surprised to find a Book of Mormon. Why someone like Mr. Landry would own such a book was beyond her. She reached out a hand and reverently touched the leather spine. Her fingers came away with light dust.

"What are you doing?" Eric's booming voice startled

her out of her revelry. Belle turned around quickly. Eric stood there glaring darkly at her. *Busted.*

"I'm sorry. I was trying to find the right room," she stammered.

"Does this look like a bedroom?" he asked. His voice thickened with anger.

Belle shook her head and tried to think of a way out of this dilemma.

"I have no problem going back on our deal. I still have the number for your father's employer on my desk," he threatened.

"No, please," Belle said. She picked up the forgotten suits and swallowed her pride while gathering her courage. "Could you please show me which room?" she asked as sweetly as she could.

He studied her for several moments before leading the way out of the room. Belle followed him, trying to hide her relief. The room he led her to was big, richly decorated as she had suspected it would be. It was immaculate, probably because of Mrs. Haygood's efforts more than Eric's. *Although he doesn't strike me as the messy bachelor kind of guy either.*

Eric stood in the center of the room and indicated the closet wordlessly. Belle tried to focus on the task at hand and not let the lavish furnishings of the room distract her.

She opened the door to find a closet big enough to rival some of the bedrooms in her family's home. Quickly she found the empty holes where the suits and shirts belonged. Everything was hung neatly on cedar hangers, sorted by color and style. Suits on the left, dress shirts on the right, with more casual polo shirts and slacks in the back of the vast closet. His shoes were lined up on racks on the floor, sorted as neatly as the clothes. There was no stray sports equipment, dirty tube socks or even so much as a t-shirt or pair of jeans to be seen. *He probably has a separate closet for really casual clothes*, she thought.

Belle finally exited the closet, feeling like a child in trouble as she waited for Eric to say something.

"I've got something for you to do in my office," he said and headed for the door.

Belle nodded and followed him out of the room, dreading whatever might be waiting for her.

"I need you to organize the files in this cabinet," he said as soon as they got back to his office. "I take whatever pertinent files with me when I travel, and over time they get out of order. Any folder that is in anyway damaged or worn needs to be replaced. You will find new folders as well as hanging files in the closet of your office. I prefer that all files be labeled with computer generated labels. I don't like trying to read people's chicken-scratch."

Belle swallowed the urge to groan aloud, and dutifully sat before the filing cabinet.

A couple of hours later, a soft knock sounded at the door. Mrs. Haygood found Belle elbow-deep in file folders and Eric typing away on his laptop.

"I have some fresh pie ready, Eric," she said with a smile. "Would you like a piece?"

Mrs. Haygood was pleased to see that Belle appeared unscathed. Eric looked up from his work and surprised Belle by actually smiling briefly at Mrs. Haygood.

"I'll be right over." The words almost came out kindly.

Mrs. Haygood turned her attention to Belle next.

"You come too, dear," she said in grandmotherly fashion. Belle smiled and nodded her acceptance. With that Mrs. Haygood turned to leave.

"Thank you, Mrs. Haygood," Belle called out after her. She glanced at Eric, surprised at how calm and almost normal he appeared to be with Mrs. Haygood. *Maybe there's more to this man. Maybe there's something kind in him that outsiders can't see.* Eric had turned back to his work. Without looking up he said:

"Go ahead."

She almost leapt from her chair. Without having to be told twice, Belle set aside the files she'd been working on and left the office. She wandered back through the hallway and found a bathroom where she could wash the dust and grime of old files from her hands.

She looked in the mirror. She took a moment to study her reflection. Her hair was slightly askew, her eyes looked tired, and her hands stung with the pain of what she was sure were a hundred paper cuts.

"Belle?" she heard Mrs. Haygood calling for her. Quickly she combed her fingers through her hair and, with one last look in the mirror, she left.

Belle walked into the kitchen and found Eric sitting at the table. He was engrossed in the newspaper and paused every few minutes to take a bite of pie. As usual he didn't acknowledge her presence. Mrs. Haygood slid a piece of steamy apple pie in front of her, along with a glass of milk.

"Here you go, dear," the housekeeper said.

"When you're finished, you can alphabetize the book collection," Eric spoke up. He still didn't look away from his newspaper.

Mrs. Haygood's movements stilled for a second. She looked at Belle and could see the girl was trying to bite back the negative remark she so wanted to spit out.

"Are you sure?" Belle asked after a moment. "I can do—"

"I want you to alphabetize the books," Eric insisted.

Belle tried to appear undaunted.

"I can handle more than filing and alphabetizing, if you want. I'm pretty organized," she said hopefully.

Eric was unrelenting. "Then alphabetizing the books shouldn't be a problem."

Belle nodded, defeated. She was right where he wanted her and she knew it. He was going to do everything he could to make this as miserable an experience as possible for her.

Mrs. Haygood intervened, trying to break the tension.

"Where do you live, Belle?" she asked.

Belle felt warmed with her interest. "A few blocks from here—"

"I'm trying to read," Eric interrupted tersely.

Belle kept quiet and Mrs. Haygood sighed. She glared at Eric reprovingly, but he was back to being engrossed in his newspaper and didn't see it. If he had, Mrs. Haygood knew he wouldn't have cared anyway.

As Belle drove home that night, she mentally reviewed her day. She'd survived it, which said something. It really could have been worse, though it could have been better too. She wondered what had happened to Eric Landry to make him into such a harsh, vindictive man. Belle pulled her car into the driveway. She wearily let herself into the house, wanting nothing more than a good meal and her bed.

When she walked in, Kelli was in the middle of cooking her specialty: spaghetti and cheese. The hope of a good meal swiftly evaporated. Belle smiled to herself.

Mike was running around the room, grabbing silverware and glasses to set the table with.

"Hi Belle!" Kelli greeted her enthusiastically.

"Hi Kelli." Belle wished she had even half of her sister's energy at the moment.

"Dad, Belle's home! Can we eat now?" Mike yelled into the next room.

Belle smiled. It didn't have the quiet solitude Mr. Landry enjoyed, but it was home.

Watson came in from the living room and gave his daughter a hug.

"Hi Dad," she said

"Let's eat," he said. He took his seat at the head of the table.

Belle slipped into the other room to put her coat and bag away. In record time the kids and the food were at the table. Belle rejoined her family as Mike and Kelli chattered loudly to each other.

"Mike, will you say the prayer?" Watson asked, reigning in the kids.

"Dear Heavenly Father," Mike mumbled, "We're thankful for the food. Please bless it that it'll taste good. In the name of Jesus Christ, Amen."

"Thanks, Mike," Kelli said sarcastically. She picked up a dish and began to pass it around.

"So, Belle, how was your day?" Watson asked. The tone in his voice was cautious.

"Yeah, was the Beast as bad as everyone says?" Kelli interjected, not nearly as cautious as her father.

"Kelli!" Belle scolded.

"Well, they all call him that. Last week in Sunday School, Sister Robertson used him as an example of pride and anger."

Belle rested her head in her hands.

"I'm thrilled to hear that," Belle dead-panned, "but it's still not nice."

"She said it's what keeps him from going to church, that and the alcohol," Kelli went on.

"That's enough, Kelli," Watson said, laying a hand across hers to get her attention.

Kelli shrugged, not sure what the problem was.

"Is he mean?" she asked with a little more reserve.

Mike chimed in. "John McCoy said Landry—"

"Mr. Landry, Mike," Watson corrected.

"—Mr. Landry chased him down the street one day," Mike finished.

"What did John do?" Watson asked.

"TP-ed his mailbox."

"That's lame," Kelli said.

"That's lame," Mike mimicked.

"Mike, stop it." Belle sighed. She snagged a piece of bread from the bread basket in the middle of the table.

She tried to ignore the conversation. She'd had enough of Eric Landry for one day and that last thing she wanted was to talk about the man. She served herself some spaghetti. With delight, she discovered it wasn't too bad.

Mike had quieted and turned back to Kelli, chattering about some friend at school. Watson watched his oldest daughter. It had not gone well, he judged.

"So how was it?" he asked again, this time a bit quieter to avoid the kids' input.

Belle shrugged. "Bearable."

Watson nodded, although he wasn't quite sure if he believed her.

Chapter Three

The next day Mr. Landry was even more difficult than before. He spent the morning reading over contracts and other business papers in the lounge. Belle walked in with the glass of juice he had requested. She placed it on a coaster on the table next to him. Before she could turn away, Eric issued another command.

"There's a phone number on my desk. I need it right away."

She nodded and turned to leave. She walked the halls quickly, for fear if she took too long he would bluntly inform her of it. Naturally his office was not only on the other side of the house from the lounge, but one floor up as well. Belle skidded to a halt in front of Eric's desk to find it littered with pieces of paper. She leafed through them until she found one with a phone number. Hoping it was the right one, she started her return journey to the lounge. She got to the lounge and handed him the paper while trying to catch her breath. He barely glanced at it and handed it back.

"No, not this one. Maybe it's on my credenza."

Belle sighed and left again at a slower run.

The days continued like this, with Eric finding every menial, mundane, brainless task he could think to give her. Belle learned to steal moments away from him when she could. One day Eric was typing at his laptop. She quickly and quietly finished straightening up some files. Seeing that his attention was otherwise engaged, she slipped out of the room. She returned to her office where she had left a textbook on her desk. She sat down and pulled the book to her, along with a spiral notebook. Belle looked around to be sure she wouldn't be caught. Then feeling safe to do so, she opened the book and began reading and making notes in her notebook.

Of course, minutes later she was interrupted.

"Belle!" Eric bellowed from his office.

She sighed, closed her homework and rose to do Eric's bidding. Belle was determined not to let Eric's sour moods affect her, but it was proving to be difficult. She worried about her homework. She was so close to finishing her degree and with finances so tight, she couldn't afford to prolong her studies any more than necessary. Unfortunately, Eric's demands left little time for Belle to fit in homework. It frustrated her that he would give her busy work when her time could be so much better spent doing things that really mattered.

One such day had her entering data from contact cards into his laptop. Belle paused in her work to look out the window. Eric stood on his basketball court in jeans and a polo shirt, working on his free throws. She watched him play a minute more and then turned back to face her work. Her textbook lay untouched on the credenza. She looked at it longingly and then with a sigh returned to the tedium of data entry.

That night Belle lay sprawled on her bed, catching up on her studies. She had made good progress in her Business Management reading. She liked to outline the chapters as she read them. Though in theory it helped her to retain what she read, it really just made her feel like she was learning. Whether or not that was true was another story. Her test scores were high enough, so she figured she was doing something right.

She was only one chapter behind when the doorbell rang. Belle ignored it, continuing her work. Kelli or Mike would answer the door. It wouldn't be for her.

Moments later, however, Kelli came bounding in.

"It's a *guy-y*," she said, stretching the word for emphasis.

"Who?" Belle asked absentmindedly.

"Craig!" she reported excitedly. "Who is he?" She acted like she had stumbled onto the secret romance of the century.

Belle sighed, and despite Kelli's excitement, she felt none. She walked past her bouncing sister and went to deal with this interruption.

Craig was sitting in her dad's favorite chair like he owed the place when Belle walked in to greet him. He stood and flashed Belle a charming, confident smile.

"Hey Belle."

"Hi," she greeted.

"I thought we could go get some ice cream."

Belle sighed. She was tired and had much to do still, but Craig looked so hopeful that she couldn't disappoint him. She mustered a smile.

"Okay."

She grabbed a jacket and followed him out the front door. As they walked to his car, Craig bounded ahead of Belle and opened the door. She was almost pleased at the thoughtfulness. But then he ducked into the car and reached for something on the dashboard. He came back out with two pints of ice cream and two spoons.

"Well, I saved us a trip," he said. He shut the door and suavely leaned against his car. He patted the spot next to him. She managed to smile as he passed her a pint and a spoon. Slowly, she settled against the car next to him.

"Thanks," Belle said.

"I was looking forward to spending time with you the other day. Why didn't you come with us?" he asked, leaning slightly into her personal space.

"I had to work," Belle replied. The pint of ice cream was cookie dough-flavored. She took a bite.

"Really? But you were just leaving work."

The confusion on his face was clear. Belle tried to explain simply. "I have a . . . second job."

Craig seemed to consider that for a moment as he stabbed at his ice cream.

"Second job," he repeated.

Belle nodded and took another bite.

"Don't you think that's a bit much?" he asked.

"I can handle it."

"But Anna said you're in school too."

"So?" she prompted, raising an eyebrow.

Craig shifted a bit. He took a bite of his ice cream—chocolate—and then smiled.

"Isn't school already like a second job? So now you have two? Or even three?" He paused and waited for some reaction or understanding to his words. "Come on, Belle. Maybe it's time to settle down and let someone take care of you."

Belle stared at him uncertainly.

"I can take care of myself pretty well." She tried to laugh it off.

"You know what I mean," Craig said. "Like a boyfriend. Or a husband."

Belle fought not to choke. She closed the lid on her ice cream and took a steadying breath. She didn't want to let him weird her out or at least not let him know that she felt uncomfortable.

"Haven't found the right guy yet," she replied, trying to

keep her voice casual.

"Maybe he's right in front of you." Craig flashed her his best charming smile.

Belle swallowed hard.

"Craig, we haven't even gone on a date yet."

"I can fix that."

He was missing the point. Belle backed up and tried again.

"What I'm saying is we hardly know each other."

"Sometimes you have to trust your feelings," he coaxed. "And if you're not sure, trust mine." He was brazenly relentless.

She took another steadying breath and handed him the half-eaten ice cream container.

"I've got to go," she said, pushing off the car. "I have an exam coming up. Thanks for the ice cream."

Belle started up the front walk.

"Belle," he called out. Belle just wanted to keep going, but politeness made her stop and look back at him.

"Where's your new job?"

She continued to the front door and paused before going inside.

"The Landry Mansion." She quickly slipped inside her house and closed the door behind her.

Belle knocked lightly on Eric's office door. After receiving no answer, she slowly opened the door and peeked inside to find the room empty of its usual occupant. Belle continued through the house, looking for Eric. She made her way to the kitchen where she found Mrs. Haygood. The housekeeper was putting together an elegant breakfast feast.

"Good morning, Belle," she said, looking up from her cooking. "Want some breakfast?"

"Uh, no, no thank you. Is Mr. Landry here?"

"Yes. He's in the spa room. He just asked for you," Mrs. Haygood replied.

"The spa room?" Belle repeated as the words registered in her mind.

Mrs. Haygood chuckled as Belle left the kitchen and made her way over to the spa room. It was a beautiful room with sunlight streaming in through the windows, casting reflective rays on the walls. Everything in the room's design was for peaceful rest. She found Eric soaking in the hot tub, eyes closed in complete relaxation. Sunlight hit his face from the skylights above and made him look almost serene. He wore only bathing trunks and this unnerved Belle. Sure, it was fine for swimming and a Jacuzzi, but this was hardly a business situation.

She thought he would notice her presence but he gave no indication of it. She felt awkward and uncomfortable invading his sanctuary, but Mrs. Haygood said he had asked for her.

"Mr. Landry," she finally said, clearing her throat.

He opened his eyes.

"Ah, Belle," he said and then shut his eyes again. Belle stood there, unsure of what to do. Then he continued. "I have a book on my nightstand, in my bedroom. Bring it to me."

He was doing it again. Treating her like she was some mindless automaton. She left to complete the assignment, swallowing the impulse to sigh loudly. Finding his room quickly this time, she headed straight for the nightstand, scowling at the idiocy of the assignment. She grabbed the book and then paused as she noticed a picture next to it. It was of Eric and an attractive woman. She studied it for a moment. He seemed happy in the picture. There was a light in his eyes that seemed to be missing now. She wondered why.

Before she could really think of it further, she remembered that she should hurry. She didn't want to risk her boss's ire.

She returned to the spa room to find Eric sitting up in the tub with an arm outstretched impatiently, waiting for the book. *What a snob.* Belle handed him the book and waited. No 'thank you' was voiced. No appreciation whatsoever.

"You can wait in the next room. Read a book, if you want," he said, dismissing her.

Belle glared at him. As she retreated, she muttered to herself, "At least I'll be able to find one easily."

She settled into a chair by the fireplace with her textbook. Glad to have a moment to catch up, she opened up to where she had left off and tried to focus enough to read. However, studying was the last thing she wanted to do. Five minutes later she gave up and looked at the shelves around her. She spotted the leather-bound Book of Mormon and opted to read it instead. She pulled it off the shelf and reverently wiped the dust from its cover.

She turned to the middle of the book and began to read.

A few minutes later, Eric bellowed: "Belle!"

With a sigh she quickly shut the book and went running to the spa room.

"Yes?" she asked, standing before him with the book still in hand.

Eric looked up at her and started to indicate the towel rack when he noticed the book. *What's she doing with* that? he wondered with a scowling look. He refocused on the towel rack.

"Get me a towel there," he demanded.

Belle noticed nothing in his mood change. Then again he always seemed to be moody so a change would be difficult to perceive. Setting the book down on a nearby lounge chair, Belle crossed the room to the rack. She handed the plush, luxurious towel to Eric and was surprised when he didn't immediately take it. He stood, seemingly unbothered by his physical dress. Belle blushed; what she would have given to be anywhere but there. She unfolded the towel and held it out to him at arms length. He sloughed off the excess water from his chest and arms. He ran his fingers through his hair, pushing it back from his face. Finally, after several agonizing moments, he took the towel and began to dry off.

"What are you doing with that?" Eric asked. He nodded at The Book of Mormon with obvious disgust.

Belle was confused and surprised at his reaction to the book. *Maybe it's some family heirloom or something*, she thought.

"Reading. It was on your shelf—I hope you don't mind."

"Get rid of it," he said almost bitingly. He was reacting like it was the plague or something.

"What? Why?" *Where's this anger coming from?*

"I said, get rid of it!" Eric nearly yelled.

"But it's a nice copy," Belle protested.

Eric angrily grabbed the book from her hand and threw it into the spa water. Belle gasped.

"What—how could you . . ." she stammered. Her heart beat rapidly in her chest, aching with the disrespect that Eric so blatantly displayed.

"It's just a book."

He dropped the towel and picked up his robe from a nearby lounge chair, glaring at her as he draped it over himself.

"No, it's scripture." She said it with the conviction of her soul, but on Eric, it had no effect. He rolled his eyes, his heart hardening even more and the corners of his mouth turning up maliciously.

"Isn't that sacrilegious?" Belle tried again, pointing to the almost drowning book.

"Do you think I care? I haven't cared what God thinks for years."

"Well, maybe that should change." She knelt down by the tub's edge and defiantly reached in to rescue the water-logged book. She stood back up and began to dry the book with the discarded towel.

Eric saw the hurt in her eyes. She seemed almost heart-broken over what he deemed a waste of space. He pushed the thought aside and continued to glare at her insolence. She faced him full on now, an angry challenge in her eyes. He noticed the breath she took to calm herself before she spoke.

"I don't know you or your reasons and you don't know me or mine. But please, don't be so disrespectful."

"It's my house," Eric taunted her. "If you don't like it, you're welcome to leave."

Belle tried not to groan aloud, knowing she really didn't have that choice. She had to stay for her family's sake.

"Then deal with it," he said. "I'm going out of town tomorrow. In my office is a list of things for you to do while I'm gone. For now, go pack my bag for the trip."

No 'please,' no 'thank you,' no 'I'm sorry.' He just moved on and gave her another order. To Belle, Eric's arrogance knew no bounds. She gawked at him as he walked out of the room, seemingly carefree and unbothered by his behavior.

"Mrs. Haygood," he called out, "what's for breakfast?"

Belle finished drying the water drops from The Book of Mormon. She put it carefully in the sun to air it out, all the while wondering if Eric really was delusional enough to think his abundance of money gave him the right to be so rude and disrespectful. On her way to Eric's bedroom Belle stopped by her office and grabbed her cell phone. She hit speed dial and walked to the bedroom as she waited for someone to pick up.

"Thompson Orthodontics, this is Linda," the receptionist answered.

"Hi, Linda. Is Anna there? I have to talk to her right now."

"She's just finishing up with a patient, Belle. Can you call back?"

"No, I'll wait for her," Belle said, feeling herself get more and more agitated.

"Okay, hang on," Linda said.

In Eric's bedroom, Belle spotted a suitcase laid out and grabbed it. She put it on the bed and started pacing around the room. *Pack my bags*, Eric had said. She was his assistant, not his maid. She saw some clothes peeking out of a drawer, some slippers and shirts in his closet. Without any thought about whether Eric would actually wear these on a business trip, she grabbed them and started towards the luggage.

"Hey Belle, what's up?" Anna cheerily answered.

"I can't stand him!" Belle said as she began throwing the clothes and things into the suitcase. She went around the room again, gathering more things and angrily chucking them in the suitcase.

"Whoa, whoa. Who? What are you talking about?"

"Eric Landry," Belle replied through clenched teeth.

"Landry? As in scary Landry, Landry Mansion, scary-rich Landry?" Anna gushed.

"Yes to all."

"What are you doing around him?"

Belle took a deep breath.

"Dad broke something at Landry's when he was repairing a fireplace, and Landry threatened to call Dad's boss and have him fired, so now I'm working for Landry until he thinks he's been paid back enough." She waited for Anna's reaction.

Anna was quiet. *Did we get disconnected?*

"Wow. Is that where you've been lately?" Anna asked. "'Cause Craig thought you were avoiding him."

"No, of course not, that would be mean," Belle said.

"So, is his house amazing?" Belle shook her head—of all the questions!

"Anna!"

"Sorry. Would your dad's boss even fire him?" Anna quickly steered back to the topic.

"He's still fairly new to the job, more so than anyone else. And with Landry calling . . ." Belle sighed.

"Got it. So what's bugging you now?"

"He's a complete jerk! He's purposely making everything harder than it has to be. He has me doing menial tasks, he insults me constantly, and he has no respect for . . . for . . . anything!" Belle vented. She dropped a pair of slippers into the suitcase, right on top of a nice, pressed shirt. She didn't care if it got wrinkled. *Serves him right.*

"Guess all the rumors are true," Anna said. "You know he's a drunk, right?"

"Yeah," Belle said as she pulled socks from a drawer and threw them in the open bag. "I know everyone says that, but I haven't seen him drink yet."

"Well, it sounds like he acts like a drunk."

"This is so helpful, Anna."

"Fine. Dish it back, then. If he's going to be a jerk, show him up." Belle considered the suggestion for a moment, but then shook her head.

"I have to get through this," she said with a sigh. "I can't tick him off and then have him fire me *and* call my dad's boss."

"Then prove to him you can do more important stuff," Anna said. "What's he do, anyway? I heard he got drunk at work and started a fire."

"He's a consultant or something. I don't know."

Anna laughed. "Maybe you should find out, or he won't have any reason to trust you with something important."

"Yeah. Maybe." Belle stopped her frenzied packing and

thought for a moment about what Anna was saying.

"Want to go catch a movie? Blow this off?" Anna offered. Belle smiled. A movie sounded great, but reality prevented such an escape.

"No," she said, not able to hide the disappointment. "He's going out of town for a couple of days, but I still have tons of trivial things to do for him. Plus, school work."

"Lucky you. Hang in there," Anna encouraged. Belle appreciated her friend's support, but she couldn't help thinking what she wouldn't give to switch lives for a little bit. She smiled, despite everything.

"Thanks. See you later."

"Bye."

Belle stared at her phone thoughtfully, replaying everything that Anna had said through her mind. Maybe Anna was right. Since knowledge is power, she would take advantage of Eric's being gone and do a little research. Then maybe she could make the best of this awful situation.

Chapter Four

The next day Belle sat in the living room, surfing the Internet on the family computer. She opened up her usual search engine and typed 'Eric Landry' in the search window. She was waiting for the results to come up when Kelli walked through the door.

"Belle, you're home!" Kelli said with some surprise.

"Yeah."

"I thought you'd be at the mansion."

"You say that like it's grand and exciting," Belle said with a laugh. "Mr. Landry's out of town."

"Oh. So what are you doing?"

"Learning more about his business." Belle scanned the list of results her search brought up. Kelli stood behind her, peering over her shoulder.

"Do you think he's really out of town?" Kelli asked. "I mean what if he has a double life? Like Batman!" *How cool would that be!*

Belle tried not to scoff, for her sister's sake.

"Uh, not likely," Belle replied as evenly as possible.

"How do you know? Have you followed him?"

"No, and I never will." Belle could think of nothing she'd rather do less.

"But you could be his sidekick—Bat Girl!" The images of fighting crime with attitude and a cape were obviously flying through Kelli's mind.

"Kelli," Belle started, hopefully bringing her sister back to earth, "I'm trying to work."

"Fine," Kelli relented, "but if he ends up having a secret identity, you have to show me the Bat Cave."

Kelli walked to the kitchen. Belle tried to refocus on the computer screen without laughing. Even so, she couldn't suppress a smile.

She spent the rest of the afternoon pulling up articles and scanning them for information. She wanted so much to get Eric to take her seriously. Belle knew she shouldn't care what he thought, but she still did, if for no other reason than to be given more to do than pick up the guy's dry cleaning.

While he traveled, Belle worked through the list of tasks Eric had left for her. She quickly found that when he wasn't on the premises, it wasn't so bad to be at the mansion. Mrs. Haygood was a kind, friendly presence, and with Eric gone, Belle actually found herself admiring the decor and peacefulness of the mansion.

But two days later, he was back in town. Belle left for work at the mansion with a little trepidation.

Belle dropped her purse on her desk and made her way to Eric's office. She walked right in, determined not to let Eric intimidate her any more—but she found the office empty. She went back to the kitchen, peeking in rooms along the way. *Where is he?* she wondered. Movement from outside caught her eye. A look out the kitchen windows revealed the object of her quest, strolling along calmly. She watched him for a few minutes. Through the glass, though not rose in color, he seemed almost like a nice, warm, normal kind of person. How she wished that could be true. He hadn't seemed to notice her scrutiny. Wanting to keep it that way, Belle backed away from the windows and went back to the office.

She sat in a chair in front of his desk and waited for him to come in. When a few minutes passed and he still had not made an appearance, Belle began to look around the office, giving it a closer inspection. His chair appeared to be of fine reddish-brown leather and the desk, credenza, and file cabinets were all made of fine, polished cherry wood. A Persian rug lay on the center of the floor. The two guest chairs in front of the desk were upholstered in a rich burgundy stripe pattern and two silver floor lamps finished the look. There wasn't the artwork she had expected him to have, the obligatory portrait of his stern-looking father or some other long-dead relative. In fact, there were no paintings in the office at all. Instead there were several framed photographs, mostly landscapes and other nature shots.

Belle's eyes finally rested on the desk in front of her. She spied a report of some kind on the top of the pile. It was opened, and she read it upside down for a minute. She eventually picked it up and began to read it in earnest. The sound of a door closing interrupted her reading. Report in hand, Belle went to see who had come in.

Mrs. Haygood set the groceries on the kitchen counter. She removed her coat and hung it on the back of a barstool.

"Hello? Eric?" Belle called out.

"It's just me, dear," Mrs. Haygood replied. Belle came into the kitchen and smiled when she saw the housekeeper.

"Oh, hello, Mrs. Haygood. Can I help you with those?" Belle asked, noticing the bags of groceries.

"No, thank you. I'm okay," the housekeeper said. "Why don't you have a seat and I'll get you something to eat."

"Oh, I'm not hungry, but thank you anyway."

Belle took a seat at the counter and continued reading the report. Mrs. Haygood began unloading groceries and filling up the refrigerator. She had to smile at Belle's bravery—she knew the young woman was reading something of importance to Eric's business. And Belle was so engrossed in her reading that she didn't hear the door open again.

Eric strode through the back door, feeling quite refreshed. He enjoyed his walks. He did his best thinking while walking outdoors. He was still mulling over his thoughts when he came through the kitchen. Eric stopped suddenly upon seeing Belle with his report.

"Welcome back," Belle said, looking up at her boss.

"What are you doing with that?" he asked, ignoring her greeting. He nodded at the report.

"Reading," she replied, not backing down. "You have a typo on page 4."

Eric never tolerated insolence. This was his home, his domain and no one talked to him like that on his grounds. Angrily, he took two steps toward her and tore the report out of her hands.

"What gives you the right?" he asked furiously.

"Mr. Landry—"

"Call him Eric, dear," Mrs. Haygood interjected.

Both Eric and Belle looked at Mrs. Haygood in surprise. *Is everyone turning on me today?* he wondered. He glared at his housekeeper a moment more and then returned his glare to Belle. Mrs. Haygood stood there innocently, smiling as always. Nothing fazed her.

"Eric," Belle started, "it's my job—"

"Your job is to do what I tell you!"

"Despite what you may believe, I can think for myself!" Belle argued. She took a quick breath, calming herself for a moment. "If you really want to have a decent assistant, let me do more that run errands for you."

Eric stared hard into her eyes. "You think you know anything about what I do?" he said.

"I'm beginning to. You help companies identify problems so they become more profitable. For example, you think the company you wrote this for is way understaffed."

He stood there for a minute as if considering her words. She at least hoped he was. Eric turned away abruptly.

"I don't have time for this," he said, and he left the room.

Determined to get through to him, Belle followed Eric out of the kitchen. He continued at a fast pace to his office, trying to leave her behind. Belle matched his pace.

"Look, I might as well do something more useful," she said. "You only have so many shirts I can take to the cleaners."

Eric turned into his office, glaring over his shoulder at her. "I can buy more."

"What do you have to lose?" Belle challenged. "I'll still do the menial stuff. Just give me a chance to show you what I can do."

"You've been here a couple of weeks and you think I'd trust you with something important?"

"If you want me to be a real assistant, yes." She held her breath as her words sunk in. The clock on his desk was all she heard for a few seconds as Eric thought it over.

"Fine," he spat out finally.

Eric quickly gathered various folders and documents from his desk and then turned sharply to face her.

"Read all of these. When you start to understand what you're really dealing with, we'll talk." He said it with finality and stormed out of his office.

Belle almost giggled with happiness at the turn of events. Hugging the pile of folders to her chest, she turned and left the oppressive office, looking for a less confining place to read. She curled up by the fireplace in the sitting room and began going through the reports Eric had given her.

It didn't take long before she was lost in the reading. It was all fascinating to her, and it was a relief to be doing something that made her think for a change. She was so absorbed in it all, though, that she didn't see Eric walk by.

He was just stretching his legs for a moment when he noticed her. Belle was reading by the fireplace. She just finished one report and seemed to be considering it before going on to the next one. *Whatever*, he thought, shaking his head and continuing on his way.

Belle read for another hour and then, feeling stiff, decided to take a break. She walked through the kitchen. The creak of a chair drew her past the main kitchen. She followed the sound to a small, less opulent, white kitchen. Mrs. Haygood sat sewing at a nearby table.

"Oh, I didn't know this was back here," Belle said, coming fully into the room.

"Yes. This is the staff kitchen," Mrs. Haygood said with a smile. *Staff kitchen?*

"Aren't you the only staff?" Belle asked.

"I didn't build the place," she replied with a shrug.

Belle smiled. She liked this woman. Although how the housekeeper kept herself so cheerful living around Eric, she didn't know.

"Sounds like you've been keeping busy," Mrs. Haygood said.

"Yeah." Belle sat in a chair opposite Mrs. Haygood.

"There's been lots of shouting since you've come," the housekeeper went on.

"I imagine you'd hear that even if I wasn't here."

"Yes," Mrs. Haygood chuckled, "but that's just how he is."

She continued sewing as Belle considered her words.

"Mrs. Haygood," Belle started hesitantly, "if it's not wrong of me . . . why is Eric the way he is?"

The kindly lady smiled. "I'm sure you've heard the rumors."

"Well, yes. There are plenty, but I can't believe that more than half of them are true."

They shared a laugh at that and then Mrs. Haygood answered.

"He got married, about ten years ago. He'd started a company with two of his friends, and it was a big success. He went to church and was as strong as anyone else—he served a mission, you know. Some place in Europe."

Belle frowned, trying to imagine Eric as a missionary. *Bet he spread all kinds of joy with his charming personality. His poor companions, being stuck with him 24/7.*

"But then his wife died—Sarah was her name. It was an accident, but Eric took it pretty hard." Mrs. Haygood sighed. "He blamed God for it. No one could console him. And soon, he stopped going to church. Then he started drinking."

"So that part is true," Belle said, understanding dawning in her mind.

"Alcohol affected Eric enough that his business partners —so-called friends—ousted him from his own company. He was fine financially of course, as you can tell," she said, indicating the room with a sweep of her hand. "But it only made things worse. He was drinking so much; his whole life was out of control."

Belle sat still, entranced by Mrs. Haygood's story. She frowned as she thought about her time with Eric so far.

"But I haven't seen him drink at all since I've been here," she said, confused.

"Well, it got so bad, he finally checked himself into one of those rehab clinics. He hasn't had a drink in five years." Belle didn't miss the almost proud, motherly look on Mrs. Haygood's face. "Hard times, but he's pulled through pretty well, considering. Built himself a good consulting business and all. It keeps him busy."

"Then why is he so . . ." Belle began.

"Mean?" Mrs. Haygood filled in. "Everyone takes hard times differently. For Eric, he still blames God. And all the rumors about him don't help either."

Belle looked away, her mood somewhat somber as she digested all that Mrs. Haygood had said. She glanced at the clock and realized she had to be at the orthodontics office soon.

"I should go," Belle said as she got to her feet. "Thanks for . . . talking with me."

Mrs. Haygood smiled and Belle went back down the hall toward the office. She walked in to find Eric on the phone.

"I should have time then," he said to the caller. He looked annoyed that she was there, but did not interrupt his call to tell her so.

"Just a couple of days, to start. If we need more, we'll talk then," he continued.

Belle waited patiently for him to finish. She had stopped in the sitting room on her way to the office to gather the reports she had been reading. She stood there as he concluded his call, with her arms full of the folders.

"Okay. Bye, Mark." Eric hung up the phone and then made a note on a nearby pad of paper. He seemed to be ignoring her again.

"Eric?" she asked when she could wait no longer.

He stopped his pen mid-stroke, but did not look up.

"I have to go to my other job now," she said softly.

He glanced at the little clock on his desk.

"It's 2:15," he said suspiciously.

"I have the ending shift. And I have class after that," she explained.

"Fine," he relented with a dramatic sigh.

"If it's all right, I'd like to take these home to read tonight," Belle said, indicating the reports in her arms.

He glanced at the stack she held.

"I'm a little busy here, Belle. Do you think I care?" he said with a snort.

He continued to scrawl notes on the legal pad and Belle watched for a moment before finally giving up and leaving the room with a sigh.

However, Mrs. Haygood's story still rang in her ears as Belle left.

Chapter Five

After a long shift at the orthodontics office and a questionable dinner prepared by Mike, Belle dragged her tired body to her room. She still wanted to read through more of Eric's reports, so she took a quick shower to revitalize herself. After changing into comfortable pants and a t-shirt, Belle sprawled out on her bed and began to read.

The ring of her cell phone interrupted her reading a few minutes later. She reached over and answered the phone, not taking her eyes off the report.

"Hello?" she answered.

Outside Belle's house, Craig sat in his car.

"Hey!" he said when Belle answered.

"Hi Craig. What's up?" Belle said absentmindedly.

Craig got out of his car and started up the front walkway.

"Want to go out for dinner?" he asked enthusiastically.

"I already ate, but thanks," Belle said apologetically.

Never one to give up, Craig tried a different way.

"How 'bout a movie? Anna's been wanting to see—"

"I can't tonight. I'm in the middle of something. But maybe this weekend," she said.

Craig stopped, a few feet from the door as she explained.

"Oh, okay," he said, a little disappointed. "What are you doing?"

"Reading."

"You're going to blow us off for a book?" Craig asked incredulously.

"Work, actually," Belle said.

Craig sighed.

"All right . . . if you're sure," he finally said as if that would give her one last chance to change her mind.

"I appreciate the invite, Craig, really, I do," she said.

"Okay." Craig turned back towards his car dejectedly.

"See you later," Belle said and hung up.

Belle tossed her phone on her bed. At that moment, Kelli came bounding in through her bedroom door.

"Was that Craig?" she asked.

Belle sighed and shut the report. At this rate she was never going to get anything done.

"Yes, Kelli."

"Is he a good kisser?" the teen asked.

Belle nearly jumped at the suggestion.

"Kelli! We aren't even dating!"

"Yeah, but he's cute." Kelli tilted her head in thought. "When you kiss a guy, how do you . . . you know, coordinate everything?" she asked.

Belle blinked in surprise and discomfort. It was times like these she really missed her mother.

"I mean, does the girl tilt her head to the right, and the guy to the left?" She moved in a kind of pantomime of what she was describing. "Or are guys on the right and girls on the left? Wait . . . whose left . . . "

Belle stared at her in disbelief.

"Are you really asking me this?" she asked.

"It's a good question!" Kelli retorted defensively. "I mean, how do you not hit your heads? And what about your noses?"

Belle stood and walked towards Kelli.

"You're not going to show me, are you?" Kelli asked a little nervously.

"I'm kicking you out of my room."

Kelli quickly got out of the way as Belle shut the door.

"So, you haven't kissed Craig then?" Kelli's voice came through the door.

Belle laughed and shook her head, then resumed reading the report.

The next morning Belle found Eric in the theater room, watching some sort of DVD presentation. She stood in the doorway and knocked on the door behind her to get his attention. Eric paused the DVD and waved her in.

"Did you finish reading the reports?" he asked.

"Yes."

"Okay. Tell me what you learned." His tone held the patience of a cab driver. Belle cleared her throat.

"I thought your analysis was pretty good," she said, thumbing through the papers in her hands.

"That means so much to me," Eric muttered.

Belle ignored his attitude and pressed on.

"You're really smart."

Eric blinked, surprised at the compliment.

"I mean, I figured you had to be intelligent to do what you do, but what you've figured out and written . . . you have to be really smart," she continued.

He was so taken aback by her remarks that it took him a moment to recover his attitude.

"Now that we've established I'm smart, what did you learn?" he asked. Belle quickly looked back to her papers.

"Um, well, obviously the companies come to you for

recommendations on how to be more efficient, and to increase their profits. And based on what you wrote, they all can improve."

"They'll be thrilled to hear that," he said, sarcasm dripping from his lips.

"You find flaws that I've never thought about— "

"Not surprising," he cut in.

"—and your analysis makes my head spin," Belle said, "with revenues and cutting back debt. . . . I'm just a little confused about your recommendations though."

Eric narrowed his eyes and leaned back in his plush theater chair.

"Really?" he deadpanned.

"It seems like you're a little harsh on them. I'm wondering why. I mean, you're supposed to help them," she went on.

Eric felt his hackles rising defensively. *How can she presume to tell me about my business?*

"I *am* helping them. I tell them what they're doing wrong."

"Well . . . shouldn't you be nicer?" she suggested.

"My clients don't pay me for fluffy compliments."

"Well, that's obvious." She snorted.

Eric couldn't believe she dared to say these things. He was stunned into silence by her gall. Belle noticed and quickly continued on.

"Um, you focus on the company as an entity, right?" she asked. Eric swallowed his displeasure momentarily.

"Right."

"But it's run by people. Those people are influenced by emotions. Wouldn't it help to be a little more diplomatic?"

Eric finally found his voice. He'd had enough.

"You read a few reports and you think you know it all," he said with a smirk. "That's enough. Shut the door behind you."

Belle took a step back. She thought she was finally getting somewhere with Eric. Now it seemed she had lost any ground she had gained.

"Eric, I'm just—" she stammered.

"I don't care!" he yelled. "You don't know what you're talking about."

He stood up quickly and stalked towards her, forcing her to back up until she hit the door frame. Eric pushed her out and slammed the door behind her. He turned his back on the door and looked to the floor. The reports Belle had been holding had fallen, scattered all over.

Belle stood outside the slammed door, taking deep breaths to try to get her heart to return to a normal rhythm. Defeated, she walked back to the office and began to tackle the other tasks he had left for her.

Where did I go wrong? She couldn't lie to him about what she thought, but maybe that's what he wanted. *He's used to everyone bending over backwards to please him.* But that wasn't her style. She wouldn't lie to him just so he wouldn't become angry.

Belle sighed. She sat quietly, filing documents with little enthusiasm. She wished that things with Eric had gone better. She would be doing mindless tasks for the duration of her sentence here, she was sure.

The quiet was interrupted when a door slammed somewhere in the house. Belle peeked out into the hallway and saw no one. She listened and could hear what could only be Eric stomping through the house. She followed the sound to its source, carefully peeking in one room.

She found him working out at a furious pace in the exercise room. Before she could say a word he spotted her. He grimaced and looked away again. Belle shrank back a step.

"You're done for the day," he said coldly.

Belle tried not to flinch. She didn't want him to see that

he had affected her.

"Pick up my shirts from the dry cleaners on your way in tomorrow."

She wanted nothing more than to go home, crawl into her bed with a box of chocolate truffles and cry. Struggling to stay in control, Belle stayed a moment longer. Then with a nod she left.

She didn't notice Mrs. Haygood watching from the stairwell. The housekeeper held a basket of laundry in her arms, and though it was heavy, she'd stopped to observe Belle's retreat. Mrs. Haygood sadly shook her head, and continued down the stairs.

Belle was still going over the whole conversation in her head as she drove to the orthodontics office that afternoon. She wondered if she could fix this. *No, it's beyond damage control now.* She got to work, though, and thankfully was swept away in a flood of patients. She was glad for the distraction.

Three patients were in chairs, keeping Anna and Belle on their toes as they juggled the work.

"You're quiet today," Anna said as they got supplies for their respective patients.

"I'm working," Belle responded softly.

"Ah. Speaking of . . . how's your other boss?"

Belle tried to ignore the question. She didn't want to discuss this.

Getting no response, Anna continued, "You sure it's worth it? I mean, your dad could find another job eventually."

Belle shot her a pained look.

"We can't go through that right now. It took months for him to find this job, and with James on his mission and Kelli and Mike . . . " Belle sighed. "We need the stability."

"What about you? You're the one who's dealing with the Beast."

"Don't call him that," Belle said a little more sharply than she meant to. "He deserves a little respect, even if . . ." She shook her head.

Anna was surprised at Belle's defense of Eric Landry. She turned back to her patient, but kept looking over at Belle. Her friend looked tired, and the stress was very evident on her face.

"Want me to take Taylor?" Anna asked helpfully.

"Thank you," Belle said with a nod.

Later that evening, Mrs. Haygood found Eric working in his office. His workout had done a lot to calm him down. He sat freshly showered and crisply dressed behind his desk.

"Good evening, Eric," Mrs. Haygood greeted.

"Yes, Mrs. Haygood?" he asked.

Mrs. Haygood had an armload of files and reports.

"I found these in the theater room. Do you want them in here?"

Eric stared at the paperwork for a moment. The memory of the confrontation with Belle ran quickly through his mind.

"Uh, yes," he finally said.

She studied him carefully, gauging his mood.

"Dinner is nearly ready. Is Belle still around to join us?" she asked, keeping her tone light.

"Do you see her here?" He squinted at Mrs. Haygood, wondering what she was up to.

"Just wondering. She must have left earlier today."

Eric frowned.

"What are you getting at?" he asked suspiciously.

"Oh, nothing," she shrugged. "Don't be too long or the food will get cold."

"I'll be there in a few minutes," he replied, refocusing on his work.

Mrs. Haygood set the pile of folders on a corner of Eric's desk, just on the edge of his eyeline, and then left to finish dinner.

Eric tried to focus on his work, but his attention kept wandering to the files. With a sigh, he picked the top report off the pile and began paging through it.

The next morning Belle braced herself for an unpleasant day at the Landry mansion. She reached into her car and pulled out a large number of freshly laundered, plastic-covered dress shirts. Stopping at the front door, she took a deep breath and then walked on in. Belle went straight to Eric's bedroom. She thought back to when she first tried to find it and almost blushed at the memory. She walked right through the bedroom, the sitting area and into the closet. She quickly put all the shirts in their appointed places and then took a minute to straighten everything up before walking back out.

Belle gasped. Eric was still lying in his bed. She froze, not sure how to react. Worse still, she realized he was awake and had been watching her from the moment she walked in with a measure of amusement.

"I'm so sorry. I thought you were in your office already. I'm sorry, I should have checked or . . . " she babbled.

He raised an eyebrow questioningly and pulled himself into a sitting position.

"Good thing I wasn't in the shower."

Belle blushed, wishing for a hole to open up in the floor and let her fall through.

"Um, I'll wait in your office," she said, rushing to the door.

"I'm taking the day off."

Belle paused in her mad dash.

"I'm not feeling terribly well," he explained, running his hand through his bed-head somewhat bashfully.

"Um," Belle started, "do you want me to get you something? Or Mrs. Haygood, or your doctor?"

"My doctor?" Eric asked with confusion. "What do you think is wrong with me?"

"Nothing, I just thought . . . never mind," she said, feeling the embarrassment creep into her face.

Eric gave her one of his analytical looks. She disliked the scrutiny. It made her want to squirm.

"What?" he finally asked.

Belle sighed. "Well, I figured you'd have one on hand or something."

"Why's that?"

Belle shrugged shyly. "It fit—a big house, well-off guy, the doctor on retainer." She paused. "Maybe it's just a movie thing."

"Maybe," he agreed.

Belle was now thoroughly embarrassed and turned to leave.

"Belle," Eric called out.

She turned around and looked at him cautiously. Eric took a breath as if trying to compose himself. Belle frowned; he was usually so confident and together.

"I'm sorry for my behavior yesterday," he said, and for Belle, time stood still. "You, um, read everything, and I . . . " He cleared his throat. "Anyway, my apologies."

Belle was stunned. She never expected this from Eric of all people. An awkward silence reigned. Eric waited anxiously for some kind of response, acceptance or otherwise.

"Feel free to take the day off," he said as if to sweeten

the apology.

"Uh, okay." She snapped out of her stupor and began to high-tail it out of there before things got anymore awkward. She reached the door but stopped.

"Thank you," she said softly with a smile. Eric nearly smiled back.

"See you tomorrow," he said. She left.

Eric slid back down under the covers and with the load of guilt off his conscience, soon fell into a deep peaceful sleep.

Chapter Six

Belle sat in the office the next day, waiting for Eric to come in with the day's task list. She walked slowly by the bookshelf, looking at the many titles he had. Small art pieces also dotted the shelf. She admired the purple geode bookends and the collection of first edition books he owned.

A framed bottle caught her eye. It seemed strange to her that a person would frame a bottle. Upon closer inspection, Belle realized that it was a whiskey flask, and it was half-empty. It was made of blue glass and sat in a brown wooden box, enclosed behind a glass pane.

Eric walked into the office, actually looking forward to working with Belle for a change. But then he saw where she stood, staring at his flask, her back to him. His mood shifted, like a fast moving thunderstorm rolling in over a sunny day. She turned her head to the side and he knew she was aware of his presence. He fought to keep his anger in check. By the time she had turned fully around, Eric managed to paste a neutral expression on his face.

"Can I ask . . . " Belle started, pointing to the flask, "why do you keep it?"

"Excuse me?" he replied, his temper flaring despite his efforts to control it.

"Isn't it kind of a temptation?"

"This coming from someone who would never understand. Have you ever had a drop of alcohol?" he asked annoyed.

Belle heard the tension in Eric's tone and worked to keep her voice calm.

"No. And you knew that. But that's why I'm asking—I really don't understand."

She wasn't judging him, Eric realized. He studied her face a moment before replying.

"It's a reminder," he explained with finality. He moved to sit behind his desk, thinking the conversation was over.

"For what?" Belle asked.

He sighed.

"For me not to go there again," he said hesitantly. He watched her as she assimilated this new information and then nodded as if his answer was acceptable.

Before he could say another word, his cell phone rang. Eric picked it up.

"This is Eric," he said and paused to listen. "Hi Kyle. Yes."

He flipped through his calendar, looking for a specific date. The office phone rang.

"The 21st should be fine. Well, the—"

He was interrupted by the office phone as it rang again. He motioned to Belle. As she picked up the call, Eric walked out into the next room to continue talking.

"Hello, Mr. Landry's office," Belle answered sweetly.

"Is Eric there?" the caller asked impatiently.

"I'm sorry, he's on another call. Umm . . . " she stalled, unsure of what to do.

"He was supposed to send me a packet yesterday, and it's not here. Where is it?" he asked, clearly upset.

Belle looked around the office in a panic. She scanned Eric's desk, not seeing anything that looked like a packet.

"Um, what's your name?" Belle asked as she searched for something to write on.

"Brent Yielding, of Yielding Dynamics," he replied in a huff.

As she dug through the papers on the desk, Belle spotted an overnight envelope peeking out from under a pile. She tugged it out and saw that it was addressed to Yielding Dynamics.

"We need that right away," Mr. Yielding continued. "I told Eric this three days ago, and he still hasn't come through, which is unlike him. I'd normally cut him some slack, but we have to present it to the board . . . "

"Actually, Mr. Yielding, it's my fault. I'm staring at the packet right now. I failed to get it out in time yesterday," Belle said. She held her breath, hoping he would accept that.

"You?"

He sighed and muttered something unintelligible.

"Your boss will hear about this," he said sternly.

"I'm very sorry. I'll take care of it right away. You'll have it in the morning," Belle promised.

"I'd better." He abruptly hung up the phone. Belle sighed and picked up the packet as Eric walked back into the office.

"Who was that?" Eric asked.

"A Mr. Yielding."

He groaned. "The packet."

"Is this it?" she asked, waving the envelope.

He nodded.

"There's no problem. I'll just take it right now, if you want." She grabbed her purse and walked out the door.

Eric frowned, upset that he'd forgotten something that important. With a sigh, he picked up his cell phone and quickly scrolled through the phonebook to the entry for Yielding Dynamics.

"Mr. Yielding, please," Eric said and then was put on hold.

~ ~ ~ ~

Mrs. Haygood was stirring some kind of sauce in a pot on the stove when Belle came back. She watched as Belle walked passed her to the office and then came back.

"Is Eric here?" Belle asked the housekeeper.

Mrs. Haygood smiled. "He's walking outside. He asked that you wait in the great room. I'll go get him," she said, lowering the heat on the burner. Belle stood still.

"Um . . . "

"Yes dear?" Mrs. Haygood asked, wiping her hands on a dish towel.

"Which one is the great room?" Belle asked sheepishly.

"The room off the entry way."

Belle frowned. "Eric's bedroom?"

"No. It's a nice room, but no need to give it an ego," Mrs. Haygood said with a chuckle. "Let me show you."

Mrs. Haygood led the way to the living room with a thirty-foot high ceiling. Rich furniture and other opulent decor and art dotted the room.

"Here we are." Mrs. Haygood gestured to the room.

"Oh. Why's it called the great room?" Belle asked.

"Because it's big."

"Everything here is big," Belle said with a laugh.

The housekeeper left her in the great room and went to find Eric. Belle sat down on the overstuffed sofa, sinking into the soft cushions to wait. She gazed out the large windows that lined the back wall of the room, lost in her thoughts.

Footsteps on the hardwood floor shook her out of her reverie. She turned to look in the direction of the sound. Eric walked in and stopped to stare at her for a moment. He began pacing, looking anywhere but at her. He seemed upset, not angry this time, but clearly uncomfortable. She watched his little anxiety dance for a moment. Finally he stopped walking and looked at her.

"You covered for me on the Yielding thing," he began.

He went quiet again. Belle wasn't sure how to respond. She couldn't tell if he wanted an explanation or an apology. Before she could ask, he continued:

"I didn't even think about it yesterday. That's what I get for taking a day off."

Belle tried to offer a sympathetic smile.

"You were sick," she said, giving him a defense.

"It's not an excuse," he said, frustrated. He paused a moment and then continued in a softer, almost kind voice. "Thank you, for what you did."

Belle tried to digest what he just said. Slowly, a smile crept over her face. Eric Landry was actually being nice; he was expressing gratitude!

Before she could say anything, Eric picked up a file folder from the mantle.

"I'd like you to read this analysis. Make it more . . . diplomatic. We can go over it tomorrow," he said, handing the file to her.

Belle took the file from his hand. Eric's change of attitude had her off balance. She wasn't quite sure what to make of it, but she liked it. Before she could even ask, Eric turned and made a hasty retreat. She watched him go and stifled a laugh as he fled the room in a controlled manner.

Belle sat, still processing what had just transpired. Opening the file, she began to read. A half hour later the grandfather clock chimed once, bringing her attention to its face. *Time to go.* She gathered the file and grabbed her purse from the kitchen counter and left the mansion.

Belle spent the evening reading through the analysis Eric had given her. On the second read-through, she made notes in the margins as she went. She got through the first five pages and then felt her eyes getting heavy. With a sigh, Belle laid the file aside and crawled under the covers.

Eric had no new tasks for her the next morning, so Belle decided to continue working on the file. In her experience at the mansion, she had discovered a narrow stairwell that led up to a rooftop terrace. The terrace had a couple of benches, large potted plants and a railing around the edge for safety. Belle found it to be a good place to think. She sat on a bench overlooking the back grounds of the Landry estate and resumed her work on the report. She finished making her initial notes and was reviewing them when Eric found her.

He came out onto the terrace and watched her for a moment without her noticing. He smiled and cleared his throat to get her attention. Belle looked up and smiled back.

Eric approached her with a paper in hand.

"What are you working on?" he asked.

She fluttered the folder in her hand.

"Oh, I'm just finishing up on the diplomacy revision," she explained. "Did you have some thing you needed?"

He did, but he let it go for now.

"You're still working on that?" he asked with a small nod to the folder.

"Yeah."

He smiled. "It's not the State of the Union. Come on," he said, reaching for the folder.

"It's not done." Belle tried to step back.

"Well, let's see what you have," he said, and he took the folder from her. He began to look over her notes.

"I'd much rather explain my notes. I just wrote whatever I was thinking," she hedged.

Eric continued reading. Belle watched as his jaw tightened and his body went rigid. His hand clenched tightly, bending the folder's edge.

"'Find the good in the manager,'" he read her notes aloud. "'Respect the CEO—he brought you in.'"

Belle cringed.

"'Too harsh,'" Eric continued. "'Too critical. Too mean.'"

"Eric—" she tried to interrupt.

"'Why would they listen to criticism with no hope?'" he read aloud next. Belle shut her eyes briefly.

"I was going to type this up, explain what those notes meant," she said, dreading what he must be thinking.

"No need. They're quite clear," he said tightly.

"Eric, please—" she pleaded.

He walked to the other side of the terrace and she followed him.

"Let me finish," she said. Eric spun around, startling her.

"Finish? There's more?" he said. She could hear the hard edge of sarcasm in his voice. "Well, great, I can't wait to hear how else you think I've failed at what I do!"

"Eric, you asked me to—"

"I'm well aware what I asked! Now I'm telling you to stop!"

Eric leaned over the railing and angrily tossed the file over. The pages scattered, fluttering to the ground below.

"It's done," he said with finality. "You think you understand this business simply because you can read. *I* know my clients and what they need to hear."

Eric stormed back across the terrace and slammed the door behind him as he left. Belle looked back over the railing at the scattered pages. She sighed, and shut her eyes, composing herself. With another deep breath, she opened her eyes and made her way to the door.

Eric continued to storm through the house, down three flights of stairs to the recreation room. He grabbed a cue from the rack on the wall and began an angry game of pool. He pounded the balls ruthlessly. They bounced off the sides, refusing to fall in the pockets, which only fueled his anger.

He reset the game, arranging the balls in the center with the triangular rack. With a powerful break, the balls scattered. He jabbed at various targets with the cue stick, but his luck—or aim—didn't improve.

Frustrated, he dropped the cue stick and leaned over the table, his hands gripping the sides for support. He took in some deep breaths, picked up the fallen stick and placed it back on the wall rack.

Belle made her way down the stairs and out the back door. She walked past the tree tunnel to where the papers had landed. For a moment she did nothing, just stared at the mess, defeated. *Maybe he really is nothing more than a beast.*

With a sigh, Belle began gathering up the pages, smoothing them and placing them in the folder as she went. Some had ended up slightly impaled on the thin branches of a nearby tree. She stood on the tips of her toes and managed to pull the page off without any further damage to both page and tree. She spied the last few pages half under a bush and crawled on hands and knees to get them. She grabbed them and pulled back, sitting on her haunches to smooth out the wrinkles. Before she could rise, a pair of polished shoes entered her view. Belle pulled further back, glancing up to see

Eric's face looking down on her. She closed her eyes, steeling herself for what was to come.

"I'm sorry," Eric said.

Belle opened her eyes, surprised. He seemed sincere, but she thought that before and had been wrong. With some reservation, she stood and faced him.

"Did you have something you wanted me to do?" she said lifelessly. She was so tired of his mood swings. She just wanted to survive the experience as unscathed as possible. She watched as he fished a piece of paper out of his pocket.

"Yes, actually," he said. "Just a few things I thought you could help me with. But don't worry about it now." He handed her the paper anyway.

Belle looked over the list of tasks. They were actual business tasks, not mindless busy work. She wanted to believe this was for real and not some temporary change that would last only until his next outburst.

"I'd rather get your dry cleaning than have you yell at me for my work," she replied tersely.

He tensed at her reply, fighting to keep himself under control.

"I'm trying to be nice," he said through a clenched jaw.

She said nothing and he realized how hypocritical he sounded trying to be nice with an angry tone of voice. He paced back and forth a few times, reminding Belle of a lion at the zoo. His anger was still there, but at least it was more inward, directed at himself.

"Your notes were correct," he started again, this time more softly. "I'm just not used to criticism."

"Ironic how someone so critical can't take criticism," she said.

He looked up sharply at her. The tension was back, but with a deep breath, she saw it dissolve from his face.

"Come on," he said evenly. He held out his hand to her. Belle glanced at it, then back to Eric. Eric quickly dropped his hand, and walked ahead towards the grounds of the property.

She watched him for a moment, unsure of what to make of this. He glanced over his shoulder at her, and Belle shook herself from her stupor. She hurried to catch up to him.

He took her past winter flowerbeds, a little man-made stream, and the covered outdoor pool. She was still awed by the vastness of his estate. *How far back does this place go? What else is hidden back here?* she wondered.

"I find this," he said, indicating the grounds around them, "clears my head. I thought you might enjoy it too."

They continued walking a little further in silence. Eric truly wanted to make amends and didn't know exactly what to say. He had noticed the light that was normally in her eyes had dimmed when he exploded on the terrace. To him, she'd always seemed pretty strong-willed and this loss of spirit startled him. What surprised him more, though, was that he missed it, that light, and knew he was the cause.

"You've been working hard up there," he said tentatively.

"It's just some writing, revising . . . " she said quietly. She was not going to make this easy on him. He tried again.

"I didn't mean to disregard your work. Neither should you."

Belle didn't expect the honesty with which he spoke. She sighed.

"The grounds are very nice," she gave in.

Eric nodded and tried to hide his relief.

"My wife loved flowers, plants . . . anything she could grow. She planted most of this," he said very matter-of-factly.

Belle observed him out of the corner of her eye. He didn't speak from pity or sorrow, just regular conversation. This surprised her as had the mention of his late wife.

They walked further in silence, until Belle worked up the courage to ask a question.

"How long ago did she pass away?"

"Ten years ago," he said, and then with a mischievous glint in his eye added, "but you knew that already."

Belle stopped and stared at him. Eric grinned.

"Mrs. Haygood has a tendency to talk about my history. I'm sure she's already told you plenty I'd rather you didn't know."

Belle nodded and resumed walking. "It must be hard for you," she said.

Eric said nothing. It wasn't something he liked to think about, at least not with Belle watching. A pained look crossed his face briefly but he forced it away. They walked a little further and then Eric stopped.

"I have some calls I need to make." He had suffered enough social discomfort for one day. He turned to leave, but stopped himself. "I'm really sorry about before. I do appreciate your work."

He held his gaze steadily at her eyes, though it was the hardest thing for him. He was not used to apologizing for anything. Eric did things his way and if someone didn't like it, that was their problem. But Belle was different. Somehow he couldn't bear for her to think badly of him. She nodded her acceptance, and then Eric turned back toward the house.

Belle watched him walk down the path they had traveled until he was beyond her line of sight. With a sigh, she turned back in the direction they had been going and continued to explore his beautiful grounds. She found her way back to the stream and sat beside it, dipping her fingers into the cold water. She dabbed a couple drops on her wrists and felt a little more alert. Eric had been right; walking outside did help her feel better.

Or maybe it was the more pleasant side of him that was beginning to emerge.

Chapter Seven

A few days later Belle sat in her office. She finished a project she'd been assigned and glanced at her watch. She had just enough time before her shift at the orthodontics office to get a little studying in. She pulled her textbook and notebook out of her bag and began to read.

Eric returned to his office and was surprised to find Belle gone. He took a juicy bite of the apple he'd pilfered from Mrs. Haygood's stash that she used for pie. He knew she hated it when he did that.

The sound of pages turning and what sounded like frantic erasing caught his attention. Eric wandered in the direction of the sound. He stood in the doorway of Belle's office, silently observing. She frowned in what appeared to be frustration. His curiosity got the best of him and he quietly walked behind her. She didn't seem to notice he was there. He looked over her shoulder at her textbook.

"What's this?" Eric asked, startling her. Belle jumped and slammed her book shut. He nearly laughed.

"Sorry, it's just some homework. I finished the other things . . . "she rambled a little breathlessly.

"Calm down," he said with a smile. He reached over her shoulder and opened the book back up. He paged through it a moment and then looked at her.

"Auditing," he commented. "This is a little advanced."

"Well, it *is* grad school," she said matter-of-factly.

"MBA?" he asked.

She nodded and glanced back to her notebook. She'd been working some figures and couldn't get the problem to come out right.

"What did you do for your undergrad?" he asked, glancing at her work.

"English."

"And that didn't take you where you wanted to go?" he teased.

Belle looked up at him and smiled. He scanned the page of the notebook she had opened up and quickly saw the problem she'd been struggling with.

"You have an error here," he said, pointing to an eraser-stained figure.

"I know. I've been trying to figure out why."

Eric reached behind him for a chair and pulled it next to her. He grabbed a chewed up pencil, trying to grip it where it was still free of teeth marks. He pulled her notebook a little closer to him, still keeping it close enough that she could see.

"Your formula's wrong," he said. "Look at this." He began reworking the figures and in moments had her problem solved.

Belle was amazed and surprised. She'd been fighting with that thing for half an hour and he worked it out in mere seconds. He went further down the page and showed her other errors. They spent the next hour working on her studies.

Eric proved to be a good teacher. He was surprisingly patient when explaining something to her. She figured teaching allowed him to work from a position of power, so he didn't feel vulnerable. *Maybe not the most charitable thought*, she realized. But it was another part of him that Belle found she liked.

~~~~

As the days and weeks passed, things at the mansion seemed to get better and better. Belle actually looked forward to going to work, something she never thought would happen. And Eric looked forward to Belle coming each day. On the weekends he actually felt lonely. Monday mornings became a relief rather than the usual dread most working adults felt.

Belle found that she was given more and more responsibility. Eric seemed to approve of her work more easily and he took the time to help her with her studies when she got stuck. They began eating their meals together and when work permitted they would walk the grounds. Sometimes they talked and other times they walked in silence, enjoying the fresh air and just being in each other's company.

Mrs. Haygood noticed a welcome change around the mansion. She had not seen Eric smile so much in a long while. He seemed more at ease with himself and was kinder to her and Belle. Mrs. Haygood thought of him like a son, her own children having left the nest long ago. And like any mother, she wanted Eric to be happy.

She was delighted one day at lunch when Belle and Eric were enjoying her cooking as well as each other. She'd made meatloaf and mashed potatoes, something that might risk Eric's ire if he were in a bad mood simply because he didn't think it was elegant enough. But that wasn't the case today at all.

They were discussing a work project when Belle looked up. She noticed that Eric had some ketchup at the corner of his mouth. She laughed.

"You have—" She couldn't complete the sentence. Instead, she just reached up and wiped the ketchup away with a finger. Eric nearly blanched at that, horrified, but he quickly joined in on the laughter Belle couldn't hold back.

What also surprised Mrs. Haygood, Belle and even Eric more, was his growing tolerance to Belle's suggestions.

One day they were reviewing a company recommendation report that Eric had completed for a new client. Belle sat at his desk, scrolling slowly through the computer file, revising his comments as she went. Eric stood behind her, looking over her shoulder at what she was doing. She highlighted a passage and moved to delete it.

"What's wrong with that?" Eric asked, stopping her.

"It's condescending."

"No, it's honest. I mean if you've seen this place—"

"There's being honest and there's being excessively blunt," she teased, and promptly deleted the passage.

He crossed his arms and watched her retype the sentence into something slightly softer, but still effective. A smiled tugged at the corners of his mouth as he saw that she was right.

As the days passed and they continued to work together, they became playful around one another. Mrs. Haygood noticed that Eric seemed to come to life. She watched as he teased Belle, tossing around a stress ball in front of her while she tried to concentrate on a phone conversation she was having. Belle reached out and grabbed the ball from the air as he tossed it again. He pretended to be hurt until she tossed it back at him. He grinned.

Eric gave Belle more time to tend to her studies and even just to read. He walked by her favorite spot in the sitting room near the fireplace and saw her reading The Book of Mormon. He paused and just looked at her, admiring the serene look on her face and the peace she seemed to radiate. There was a time when he had felt that way, but it had been so long ago. He watched her a moment more and then went on his way.

~~~~

Later Belle found Eric shooting hoops on the basketball court. She hated to interrupt, especially since he looked so carefree, but someone was waiting on the phone to talk to him.

"You have a call," she piped up. Eric turned to her with a grin.

"Okay. Thank you, Belle," he said, and then tossed her the ball. Eric started down the path back to the house and turned to see Belle shoot the ball and score. He chuckled as he walked into the house.

They had been working hard one day when Eric called for a break. He stretched in his desk chair and leaned back. Belle sat across from him scribbling notes furiously. He watched her a moment and then stood and walked over to her. He put his hand on hers, stopping her writing. She looked up at him in confusion.

"Let's take a break. Come with me," he said extending his hand to help her up. She placed her hand in his, and rose from her seat. Setting her notes down, she allowed herself to be pulled out the door. Eric took her through the kitchen and down a flight of stairs to the recreation room.

"Do you play pool?" he asked, chalking up his favorite cue.

"A little."

"Care for a game?" he asked playfully.

"Rack 'em up," she replied with a laugh.

Being a gentleman, Eric let Belle break. He was surprised to see that she was a decent shot. She sunk two and then missed. Eric sunk three before an unfortunate bank off the side ended his turn. Belle sunk two more balls. She lined up her next shot. Eric stood just to the side of her. He stepped closer as she was pulling back to shoot so he could better see her shot.

"Looks good," he said. But having him that close made Belle lose focus. Her shot went wildly away from the intended pocket. Eric grinned.

"In the corner, left pocket," he indicated with his cue.

Belle decided turn about was fair play. As he leaned forward to take his shot, she followed and lightly brushed his arm. The shot went wild. He stood up and glared at her.

"What was that?" he accused in a teasing tone.

"Payback. You distracted me before. It's only fair I return the favor."

"You blatantly cheated, Belle," he said, laughing.

"You started it," she volleyed back.

"Did not. I was analyzing your shot. If I distracted you it was unintentional."

"Oh please!" Despite her objection, Belle couldn't actually appear mad at him. Eric tried to appear stern, and they glared at each other. There was no menace at all between them, but finally Belle broke and started laughing.

And that's how Mrs. Haygood found them. She stood, watching and smiling for a moment before she had to interrupt.

"Belle, there is someone here to see you," the housekeeper said.

Belle was puzzled. *Who could possibly be here to see me?* She looked at Eric. His expression was neutral, telling her nothing. He didn't seem to know who her guest was either.

"Really? Uh, okay," she finally said. Belle went up the stairs. Mrs. Haygood and Eric stared after her for a moment.

"Who's winning?" Mrs. Haygood asked.

"She is," Eric replied, smiling to himself.

"You seem happier, Eric."

He was surprised at Mrs. Haygood's comment.

"Oh, it's not a bad thing. You can't be a grouch forever. I'm just glad to see you smiling again," she said. With that, she returned to her work.

Eric thought about what his housekeeper had said. Then, his curiosity kicking in, he moved to follow the ladies and see who Belle's visitor was.

Craig walked around the great room, taking in all the decor. The elegant sofas, glittering chandeliers and shiny mirrors all seemed like too much to him. But as much as he wanted to dismiss the grandeur of Landry's home, he couldn't help but be impressed by it all. He walked a few more laps around the room and then sat on the plush sofa to wait for Belle. Moments later he heard footsteps echoing on the hardwood floors. He stood and pasted a smile on his face as Belle walked into the room.

"Craig." She couldn't hide the surprise in her voice.

"Hey!" he said, putting forth his most charming smile.

"What are you doing here?" Belle tried to keep the wariness from her voice, but it was too difficult.

"It's been awhile since we've been able to get together. I wanted to see you," he said.

"That's sweet of you, but you should see me at my home, not here."

"You're never there," he complained. "I've tried to catch you at home all week, but you're always here or studying or . . . " He trailed off at the sound of approaching footsteps, "Ah, the man himself."

The last thing Belle wanted was for Craig to have some kind of confrontation with Eric. She glanced around the room for an exit and saw the back door. The footsteps were getting closer. Belle grabbed Craig by the arm and pulled him outside, making sure to close the door behind them.

Eric heard Belle's frantic voice as she told her guest he shouldn't be there. He wanted to get a look at this guy. He moved into the great room only to see them disappear out the back door. Wanting a better look, Eric turned to the stairs and headed for the rooftop terrace.

Outside, Belle turned to Craig.

"Look, I'm sorry I haven't been around. I've just been really busy," she explained.

"I understand. I just hate to see Anna disappointed when we make plans and you have to bail."

Belle glared at Craig, seeing through his bluff.

"I see Anna at work all the time, and she's fine with it."

"All right," he said with a sigh, "well, then *I* hate to be disappointed. I just want to see you more. Get to know you. Go out for dinner. . . ."

Belled paced, trying to think of way out of this situation without hurting Craig. She looked at the ground, not seeing the observer on the terrace. Eric carefully stayed out of both her and Craig's line of sight.

"Craig," Belle tried again, looking him in the eye, "I think you're a nice guy. Anna's your cousin and I know she is trying to do us both a favor. But I can't drop everything and go see a movie with you and Anna. I can't ditch my family for dinner at some restaurant."

"So you ditch them for here?" Craig's voice rose. Belle put her hands on her hips.

"What?"

"When I stopped by the other day, your dad said he hardly sees you anymore."

Eric watched the myriad of emotions flood across

Belle's face. A part of him wanted to go down there and throw Craig off his property. Privacy was always very important to Eric and he imagined Belle liked hers as well.

"Why are you getting into my life? I barely know you and you're visiting my family?" Belle said angrily.

"I'm not," Craig quickly back-pedaled. "I'm just . . . Are you dating this guy?"

Eric's heart stopped momentarily.

Belle sighed. *What is it with this guy?*

"Because if you are, there's no way any of us can compete with Mr. Riches," Craig complained.

Eric smiled, proud that he had an edge over the competition. Of course, if that idiot really knew Belle, he would know that riches didn't really matter to her.

"You're being mean—" Belle protested.

"No, I'm not."

Belle glared at him and before she could get another word in, Craig continued.

"I just don't want to see you dragged down to his level because you're spending all this time with him," he said, softening his voice.

"His level?" Belle was incensed. "Despite what you or others think, Eric's actually a nice guy."

"Eric? That's informal," Craig said with a sneer.

"You expect me to call him Mr. Landry all the time?"

"It'd make me feel better."

Belle groaned. She steadied herself before answering.

"Anna and I call our boss at the orthodontics office by his first name all the time. What's the difference?"

"The difference is your boss here is rich and . . . and questionable, and . . . "

"Questionable?" Belle glared at him and then looked down at her watch. "I have to get back to work."

"Fine," Craig said, turning to leave. But he stopped and his eyes softened. "Just be careful. I don't like the idea of you working with this beast."

Belle's eyes flashed and she stepped towards him quickly.

"*Don't* call him that," she said, trying to keep in control. "I appreciate your concern, Craig, but I won't let you disrespect him, especially while you're standing on his property."

Eric felt oddly proud as he watched. Belle turned back towards the house and Craig left quietly. Eric flattened himself against the terrace wall to avoid being seen. The door shut behind Belle.

He walked to the railing on the front side of the house and watched Craig's car drive away. He replayed the whole conversation again in his mind and marveled at Belle's defense of him and his character.

Belle. He realized he needed to get back inside soon or he would be discovered.

Belle went back down to the recreation room and found the pool cues put up and the balls contained in the triangle frame. *Game over,* she thought.

She returned to the office, her face still a bit inflamed with her anger at Craig. Eric sat at his desk, typing on his laptop. He looked up as she walked in and noticed the color in her face. He tried to play it casually.

"Is everything okay, Belle?" he asked.

"Yeah, everything is fine," she said, perking up. "We never finished our game."

"Sorry about that," Eric said kindly, "but I remembered I have to get this report done. I need to email it to the client by the end of the day. But we'll finish the game another day, okay?"

"I look forward to it," Belle replied with a small smile. "Uh, do you need any help with that?"

"No, I think I can handle it. Why don't you make an early day of it. Go have some fun before you have to go to your other job," he suggested.

Belle was amazed, but grateful. She was tired and the idea of a nap sounded wonderful.

"Okay, I will. Thank you, Eric," she said, gathering her purse and book bag. "I'll see you tomorrow."

Eric looked out his office window and watched Belle put her bags in her car. She jumped slightly and for a minute he thought something had happened to her. Then he saw her reach into her pocket and pull out a phone. She answered the phone and he watched as a smile spread across her face when she spoke with the caller. He wondered who had called and what they had said to put that smile on her face.

She hung up a moment later, climbed into her car and left. He stared at the empty driveway a moment more and then turned back to his report.

The next morning Eric sat at his desk going through emails. A Ms. Davis needed notes and a chart from a meeting sent to her. He scoured his desk for his PDA and couldn't find it. He remembered last having it in his car. Belle sat at her desk editing his latest report and he didn't want to disturb her. He got up and went to the garage. His shoes clacked against the grey lacquered floor as he walked to his black BMW. Eric opened the door and crawled in the front seat. His PDA was wedged between the passenger seat and the seatbelt buckle. He worked to free it when he heard footsteps approaching.

"Eric?" Belle called to him.

He slid out of the car.

"Yeah."

"You going somewhere?" she asked.

He reached back into the car and with one last pull managed to free his PDA.

"No, I thought I lost this," he said, holding up the PDA for her to see.

"Oh. You have a message from Kyle Kincaid. He's waiting to hear if Thursday will work for you."

"Oh," he said and shut the car door. He stood thinking a moment. He glanced at Belle, who was looking around the garage in awe. He watched her as she admired the antique gas pump he kept on the landing and the two other luxury cars he owned.

"It's a dinner meeting, with him and the CEO," he said, getting her attention. "Are you free that night?"

Belle blinked. "What?" Eric felt his heart speed up. Quickly he thought of some explanation.

"It's a business dinner and I'd like my assistant to be there." *Sure, that's the reason.*

"Uh, yeah, I . . . I have a class, but I should be done by six o'clock."

"I'll come by to get you at seven."

"Okay," she agreed with a smile.

Chapter Eight

$\mathcal{B}$elle straightened out the front desk of the orthodontics office and cleared some space for her to work. She clicked on a patient's computer file and pulled up digital x-rays in preparation for his appointment.

"So is tonight the big date?" Anna asked, coming to stand behind Belle.

"It's a business meeting, that's all," Belle sighed.

"A business meeting you have to get dolled up for. Do you have a dress?" Anna asked.

"Of course. But it's nothing. And please don't tell Craig, because . . . " She sighed again and shook her head.

"Because he'll be jealous," Anna finished in a knowing tone.

Belle tried to think of a better explanation, but couldn't come up with one. She turned to Anna with an apologetic look on her face.

"It's okay," Anna said. "He's my cousin, but you're my friend, and I'm not going to force you to date him if you prefer someone else."

"Thanks," she said in relief. Then she caught what Anna tacked on. "It's still not a date, by the way. I don't think of Eric as anything other than my boss."

"Is he picking you up at your house?"

"Yes . . . "

"Then it's a date, or at least he thinks it is."

"No, it's logistics," Belle clarified. "I get back from my class at six and have to get ready quickly. He's picking me up on the way."

"Uh huh, right. Whatever." Anna didn't buy a single word.

Belle dashed into the house and dropped her books on the kitchen counter. Her dad stood cooking dinner at the stove. Her class had gotten out late. She had driven home as fast as she safely could. She still had time to get dinner on the table for the family before needing to get ready for the dinner with Eric.

"Sorry, Dad. Let me do that," she said apologetically.

"No, no. I can cook—it's probably good I do it anyway. You've been so busy."

"Okay, if you're sure," she said. She was a little relieved not to have to rush so much.

"Dinner should be ready in ten minutes," Watson said with pride.

"Actually," she said, gathering her things from the counter, "I have plans tonight. A business thing I have to go to."

Watson looked up from his cooking and studied his daughter a moment. His concern was evident on his face as he set down the wooden spoon he'd been using.

"Belle, are you sure you can handle all this? I mean, is school going to suffer, because we both know you've worked hard towards your degree."

"Well, I have a test tomorrow," she confessed. "But I'm doing all right. Eric actually has helped me understand some stuff with school, so I'm not behind."

He looked at her, unsure of whether to believe her or not.

"Really, Dad." She smiled and then left to get ready.

~~~~

Eric pulled up to the Watson house. He took in the modest house. It appeared to be a nice, well-maintained home and had a welcoming quality about it. He closed his car door and then straightened his tie. He wore a charcoal-grey suit and pewter-colored tie for a complete monochrome look. Satisfied with his appearance, Eric started up the walk to the front door.

Before he could step onto the front porch, Belle opened the door and walked out to meet him. His jaw nearly dropped. She wore a gown of pale blue with an empire waist cinched with a matching ribbon. Part of her hair was pulled back on top and the rest hung down in curls. She smiled at him.

"Hi," she said shyly and then made for the car.

He recovered a moment later and joined her.

"You look nice," he said, holding the door open for her.

"Thank you," she replied and then took in his sharp appearance. "It's nice to see that suit somewhere other than the dry cleaners."

He laughed, closed the car door, and then walked around to the driver's side. After he had buckled himself in, he smiled at her for another moment before starting the car. They rode in silence to the restaurant. Eric felt like talking to her, but couldn't get over the nervousness swirling in his stomach. He was grateful when, ten minutes later, they pulled into the parking lot of a quaint, yet fancy restaurant.

Eric opened Belle's door and offered a hand to help her out. She looked up at him and smiled as she put her hand into his.

They were met by the maitre'd at the door. Eric told them who they were there to meet and he led them to the table. Belle glanced around the restaurant. The atmosphere was quiet and reserved. It was so different from the restaurants she was used to—not a flying french fry or crying child in sight.

Two couples sat at their table, and they rose to greet Belle and Eric.

"Eric. So good to see you," he said as they shook hands.

"Likewise, Kyle," he replied. Eric nodded at the other man. "David. This is Belle Watson." He gestured to her.

Belle nodded and smiled, shaking the extended hands.

"Kyle Kincaid. I believe we spoke on the phone," Kyle said. "This is my date, Julie." He indicated the woman to his right.

"I'm David Bonds and this is my wife, Diane," David chimed in.

"Nice to meet all of you," Belle replied.

The introductions complete, Eric pulled a chair out for Belle. She smiled gratefully at him. He took his seat next to her.

"So, Eric, let me tell you what we're thinking. We've got a new idea for a product line, and want to shift it from . . . " Kyle began the business portion of the evening.

Diane leaned close to Belle and smiled.

"It's good to have you here. It's about time Eric brought somebody," she said warmly.

"What?" Belle asked, confused.

"He usually comes to these things alone," Diane revealed.

Belle was astonished. *Maybe Anna was right*, she thought. She looked over at Eric, who was already deep in business talk with Kyle and David. He looked up at that moment and caught her staring. Embarrassed, Belle quickly looked down at her menu.

The meal progressed as smoothly as the ideas that

were exchanged. The other two women were chatting about some designer, but Belle was more interested in the business conversation. She listened intently, mentally taking notes.

"We'll have to shut down that division and let people go," Kyle said, leaning back from the table, "but we think the new model will be worth it."

"You've factored in the costs of pensions, severance and so forth, right?" Eric asked.

"Of course," David said with a nod.

Belle was bothered by what they were going to do, but fought to keep her thoughts to herself. She could see other alternatives. She shifted in her seat and looked down at her napkin so she wouldn't show her agitation.

Eric, however, was attuned enough to his companion to notice her discomfort right away.

"What?" he asked gently.

"Pardon me?" She looked up like she'd been caught.

"What are you thinking?" he asked.

Everyone stopped talking and focused on Belle. She swallowed hard and took a moment to pull herself together.

"Well, is it worth it to let go of your current people?" she said, sounding more confident than she felt.

"Layoffs are a part of business," David replied matter-of-factly.

Eric watched Belle as she spoke again.

"But a new model is going to take a lot of manpower to produce. With some training, couldn't they easily take over the new production?" she asked.

"Or we could find new people who already know how to do the job," Kyle said, lacing his hands together. He looked to Eric for support and confirmation. Eric thought for a moment and then replied:

"Your current people could be trained. It may take a little

time and money, but you might be better off in the long run."

David and Kyle frowned, surprised at his change of attitude. Belle hid a smile behind her napkin as she dabbed it against her lips.

"You don't know our employees though," David objected. "Some are stubborn and change doesn't come easily."

"Well, it never does," Belle agreed, "but when faced with the alternative, you'd be surprised how many employees will go along with new training."

"I'm not convinced it's the right way to go," Kyle said hesitantly.

Belle smiled. "It might not be. But you wouldn't have to worry about new hires, quick turnover, and overloading your HR department. Think about how much time and money are wasted on employees who leave after an initial bonus kicks in," Belle countered.

"And new hires won't all be ready to work—you'll still have to train them on your company policies and procedures, if not further," Eric added.

Both men were quiet. They appeared to be considering Belle's words, especially with Eric's support behind them. Eric looked at Belle and nodded approvingly. She smiled back and then looked to Kyle and David, trying to gauge their reactions.

"Maybe you could look into that, Eric, when you visit our New York facility," David finally acquiesced.

"Sure."

The conversation turned to more casual matters over dessert. Then after exchanging goodbyes, the other couples left. Eric helped Belle with the wrap that complimented her gown. He grabbed his coat from the rack at the front of the restaurant and they left, walking slowly to the car.

"You did well," Eric remarked.

Belle laughed. "I don't think Kyle appreciated what I said."

"He doesn't have your compassion."

He held the car door open for her.

"Compassion's not a bad thing in business," she said defensively.

"I didn't say it was," he countered.

She smiled and got into the car. He rounded the car and got behind the wheel. He paused, gathering his thoughts and courage.

"Do you have some time right now?" he asked, looking sideways as her.

She studied him, trying to figure out what he was asking. Slowly she nodded.

Eric drove in a different direction from where they had come. He took back roads and soon the car was climbing up a canyon road. Belle felt her ears adjust to the altitude change as they went. She looked out the window at the beautiful snow-covered evergreens illuminated by only the moonlight and occasionally their headlights. The road narrowed as they climbed higher. The beam of the headlights caught the eyes of a couple of deer that dashed across the road. Eric navigated it all unfazed.

A short while later he pulled the car to a stop beside a snow-covered lake. He set the parking brake and then went around to help her out of the car.

Belle breathed in the fresh mountain air and looked around, taking in her surroundings. The lake was icy and nearly surrounded by trees. Somewhere a trickle of water was running and it seemed to add a melody to the night sounds.

They walked side by side as he led her towards a thick fallen tree.

"This is beautiful. So peaceful," she finally said. "I didn't even know this was here."

"It's hidden away enough."

Belle shivered in the crisp cold. Her dress was short sleeved and her wrap was made of the thinnest fabric. Eric saw her shiver again. He mentally berated himself for not thinking of the cold. He quickly removed his long overcoat and placed it around her shoulders.

"Thank you," she said. "How did you find this place?"

He hesitated a moment and then plunged in with an explanation.

"My wife. She used to come here to take pictures— photography was her hobby."

They reached a fallen branch and he dusted the snow off so she could sit. Then he joined her, pulling the collar on his suit coat up for warmth. They sat there in silence for a long moment.

"How did you get into consulting?" Belle asked, breaking the silence.

"I like it better than dealing with a whole company."

"Because of what happened with your old business," she figured out aloud.

Eric was momentarily caught off guard by this, but recovered quickly. *Mrs. Haygood strikes again*, he thought.

"I get to go in and fix things, without dealing with the day-to-day politics, people I don't like . . . "

"That's understandable," Belle said. "You're better off than if you had stayed there, don't you think?"

"No," he said with a laugh, "I'd have a bigger house if I was still there."

She tried to imagine what he'd do with an even bigger house. She laughed.

"But really . . . I kind of thought everything happens for a reason. It's not always easy, but someone's looking out for us," Belle said.

Eric tensed at that.

"Looking out for us?" He tried not to snort at the idea. "That implies that God wants us to be happy."

"You don't think He does?" Belle blinked in surprise.

Eric was quiet. He seemed to be stewing over something. Belle wondered if perhaps she had hit some nerve she shouldn't have.

Finally, he spoke so quietly that at first she had to strain to hear him.

"My wife and I were out one night, driving. We weren't speeding, or goofing around or doing anything dangerous," he said. "The front left tire hit the road wrong, just perfectly to blow out. And then . . . we went off the road."

His voice cracked a little, but he covered it with a cough.

"There wasn't a single other person on the road. No one to help. On a highway like that, it's pretty unusual. It was as if . . . " His voice caught again, but this time he laughed at himself. Belle clearly heard the pain in his voice.

Eric continued. "God knew exactly what He was doing. And I couldn't do a thing to stop Him. By the time I woke up, my wife—she was already gone. I prayed and I prayed, but it didn't make a difference. I sat trapped in that car, unable to move, for three hours before someone noticed. But I didn't stop praying—I figured it was the only thing I could do."

He laughed again, bitterly. "I was still stupid enough to believe she might be all right. That she might live." Eric turned away to wipe tears that came to his eyes. He drew a deep breath before turning back to Belle.

"No, I don't think God cares about me, or that He wants me to be happy," he said with finality.

She considered his words a moment.

"It's been a long time, and you still feel the same way?" she asked. "What about what's changed since then? You being stronger, growing from your experiences?"

"Growing?" he said incredulously. "I lost everything. I became a drunk—" he spat out the word, "—and had to put my life on hold before I lost it all."

Belle watched him for a moment. She yearned to reach out to him, to comfort him, but somehow she knew his pride might be hurt by that.

"Sometimes bad things happen to good people," she offered gently.

Eric looked back at her. He didn't understand how she could make excuses for God. He swallowed and stood.

"I should get you home," he said. He walked back towards the car. Belle watched a moment and then hurried to join him.

The drive back was silent. Eric seemed to be lost in thought or memories. Belle stole glances at him out of the corner of her eye. The silence felt oppressive to her. She wanted to say something but was unsure of what could really get through to him.

A little while later they pulled up in front of the Watson home. Eric made no move to get out of the car. It took Belle a moment to find her voice.

"Why did you do it on your own?"

Eric looked at her questioningly.

"I mean, there had to be someone you could have gone to, for comfort, for help," she clarified. She saw Eric's mouth twitch, almost smirking.

"There was," he replied. "A bottle."

Belle's heart sank.

"Not the best solution."

"Does it matter?" Eric asked back. "No one saw me as the same. The rumors started. I lost my business. What else did I have?"

Belle knew the answer, and knew Eric wouldn't accept it. She looked into his eyes.

"Maybe more than you realized," she said.

He watched as she got out of the car and walked to the front door as he considered her words. She got to the door and turned back to smile at him before she disappeared inside.

Eric drove home in a pensive mood. He entered his home quietly. Stripping off his coat and tie, he made his way to the great room. He stood and looked out the wall of windows at the grounds of his estate. His wife firmly in mind, Eric looked at the flowers and shrubs that she had so lovingly planted. He felt the pain all over again, as fresh as the day it began and turned from the windows to go to his office. He stood in the doorway of his office and eyed the framed flask. A part of him ached for the release it gave him, but another part revolted at the idea of ever going there again.

Eric turned and walked slowly down the hall. He entered the sitting room and paused a moment, visualizing Belle sitting in her favorite reading spot on the bench by the fireplace. He scanned the shelves and then looked back at the bench. He saw The Book of Mormon lying there. His feelings were jumble inside him as he approached the book. Fear warred with contempt and somewhere deep within himself was a longing, as if for home. Eric sighed and sat down on the bench. He leaned forward, elbows on his knees and with his head resting in his hands.

Chapter Nine

Belle walked into the office a little nervously. The previous evening they had talked about some deep things and she wasn't sure how Eric would be feeling. She peeked around the door and saw him typing away at his computer. He paused to flip a page in his planner and then resumed typing. She started to back away when he looked up, having sensed her there. She watched as his face softened.

"Hi," he said, offering her a smile.

"Hi," she said tentatively. "Do you mind if I study some? I have a test today."

"No, go ahead."

Belle smiled. "Thanks." She turned and left the room.

He watched her go and then sat back in his chair in contemplation, a small smile still on his face.

Belle chose to study in a lounge in the spa room, hoping the sun from the skylights would warm her. She looked up and noted the grey cloudy sky. *Fat chance of sunlight today*, she thought. She went back to her studies, reviewing both her textbook and notes.

Awhile later Eric strode in. Belle looked up from her books.

"How's it coming?" he asked.

"Good," she replied. A shiver ran through her body.

"You cold?" Eric asked.

She shook her head. "No, I'm okay," she replied. He

went to a nearby closet and pulled out a fluffy blanket.

"Here." He handed it to her.

"Oh, thanks," she said. She reached out to take the blanket and caught sight of his watch. *Oh no.* Belle grabbed his wrist and pulled the time piece towards her for closer inspection.

"Is it really . . . " She trailed off as she clearly saw the time. Belle checked the wall clock just to be sure.

"I'm going to be late," she said, scrambling out of the chair. In a mad rush, she started collecting her things.

Eric watched her in confusion.

"What?" he asked.

Belle didn't stop her hurried motion.

"I have ten minutes to get there before the exam starts."

A ring sounded from the vicinity of her purse. Quickly Belle dug through it and pulled out her phone.

"Hello!"

Eric watched as Belle continued to pack up her things while talking to the caller. Suddenly, she stilled her motions and gave full attention to the call.

"Kelli! What did you do?" she said and paused to listen. "No, I can't, not now! I have a test and if I don't hurry, I'm going to miss it." Belle looked so agitated, it was almost comical. Even so, Eric suppressed a laugh.

"You're going to have to 'fess up to Dad," Belle said into the phone. "I'll call him." She sighed. "Kelli, I have to go. I'll figure something out."

Belle closed her phone, stress evident in every muscle of her body. Eric frowned.

"What's wrong?"

"My sister," Belle said. "She got in trouble at school, and the principal wants someone to pick her up."

Belle sighed and set her things back down.

"I'm going to have to skip my test."

"What? Why?" Eric didn't see the logic. "What about your dad?" He knew how much her studies meant to Belle.

"Kelli doesn't want me to call him. Plus, it's really hard for him to just leave work at a moment's notice." Belle seemed already resigned to sacrificing her test.

"Well, I can pick her up." The words left his mouth before he really thought about it. He'd meet her sister, interact with her, 'bail her out' of school. *But if it will help Belle . . .*

Belle stopped in her tracks and turned around to stare at him.

"What?"

Eric strengthened his resolve.

"You have your exam. It's slow here today anyway. I'll pick her up and drop her off at your house," he said nonchalantly.

"Eric . . . I . . . are you sure?" she stammered.

He grabbed her book and purse and handed them to her with a smile.

"You better hurry."

She paused a moment. "Thank you." She smiled at him, and then ran out the door.

Eric drove up to the high school. It had been ages since he'd been in school himself. He parked in front of the building, ignoring the sign and curb that clearly delineated the area as a red, no-parking zone. He glanced at the front of the building, which looked so foreign to him. *Is this what high school looked like for me?* It had been awhile.

Once inside, he walked through the hallways, silent as the students were in class. They all looked the same and it took him a moment to locate a directory and a sign that led him to the office.

Through the glass of the office he saw a young girl sitting

to the side of the receptionist. He opened the door and glanced around the office. The only other student there was an older looking boy. He turned to the girl he'd seen first.

"Kelli?" he guessed.

The girl's eyes widened in surprise as she saw him.

"You're here to take her home?" the receptionist asked.

"Uh, yes," he replied hesitantly. "Do I need to . . . sign for her, or something?"

Kelli sighed in embarrassment and the receptionist looked at him like he was from another planet. Eric tried to remember how this was all supposed to work.

"Wait here. Our principal, Mr. Daniels, wants to speak to you," the receptionist said. She abandoned her post momentarily. Eric frowned.

"To me?" he mumbled to himself. He sighed and leaned against the doorway. A glance at Kelli caught her eying him suspiciously.

"I guess my sister sent you," she said.

He nodded and took a seat next to her.

"What are you in for?" he asked.

He watched as she scrunched up her face in a pained expression and muttered some incoherent answer.

"What?"

Kelli sighed. "Cheating."

The principal walked out of his office. He wore a brown suit, and a tie that had a pattern better suited for the '70s.

"Let's talk in my office," he said, indicating the small room he had just come from.

Eric straightened up and Kelli followed. The principal quickly motioned for her to stop.

"No, no, Kelli. You can stay here."

Eric looked back at Kelli as she hung her head and retook her seat. He looked back at the retreating principal in confusion. *He wants to talk to me?* Perplexed, Eric followed.

Principal Daniels sat behind his desk and invited Eric to sit in the chair in front of him. The principal studied Eric a moment, as if trying to figure him out.

"Mr. Watson," the principal began. Eric blinked. He opened his mouth to correct the man, but—

"No, no. Hear me out," the principal said. "I know you may want to defend your daughter. It's natural."

"No, but I'm not—" Eric tried again.

"Please don't interrupt." The principal wasn't rude about it, but Eric found his manner annoyingly polite. "We're concerned that Kelli would cheat. She has normally been such a sweet girl, a little rambunctious, but intelligent and able."

He paused, waiting for Eric to say something.

"Uh, yes," Eric stammered. What else was he supposed to say?

"Why would she cheat now? I've seen her scores, and she's always excelled. Perhaps there is something going on at home," Principal Daniels said, leaning forward as if he were to hear a grand secret. Eric barely suppressed a smirk.

"Not that I know of."

"Hmm," the principal said thoughtfully. He leaned back in his chair. He steepled his fingers in front of him and sat thinking.

The moment dragged on, and Eric glanced at his watch.

"Um, look, Mr. . . . " he looked at the name plate, "Daniels. I don't have a lot of time."

The principal sighed at this.

"I was afraid of that. Perhaps you should *make* time. She *is* your daughter."

"Clearly," Eric deadpanned.

"I've seen this a lot," Principal Daniels began. "In fact, it's one of the biggest problems we face in our schools today.

Parents just aren't making enough time for their children, and sometimes the children act out like this—cheating—to get attention."

"Well, we'll work on that," Eric said. He couldn't help a bit of condescension leaking into his voice.

"Good, good," the principal said. He stood. "*Listen* to your daughter. You'd be amazed how many problems can be solved just by that. Here at our school, we *listen* to our students, and I'm very proud of that."

The smirk just couldn't be suppressed any longer. Eric gave in and stood as well.

"Well, you should be," he said.

Eric and Kelli walked out of the office and down the hall. Neither one said anything until they were out of the building. Kelli exited the building first and plopped down on a nearby bench. Eric stood there awkwardly for a second and then reluctantly joined his charge on the bench.

She seemed agitated, and maybe a little guilty.

"Did you do it?" he asked.

Kelli shrugged. He smiled at her non-answer.

"Does your mansion really have secret passageways?" she asked eagerly.

"No, it doesn't." Eric chuckled.

Her hopes deflated, Kelli returned to the matter at hand.

"It wasn't really cheating," she said. "I couldn't remember this math formula to do this one problem, so I asked Dillon, but then Ms. Parker saw me and hauled me down to the office. Dillon didn't even tell me anything, but it doesn't matter because I know the formula—I just couldn't remember it right then, so it's not *really* cheating."

Eric felt like he needed a breath to recover from her

long, warped explanation.

"You may want to rethink your definition of cheating."

He hoped she wouldn't start rambling again. Eric wasn't sure what to think of the long chatter. The last time he really had experience with children was when he was a kid himself.

"I'm so dead," Kelli started up again. "Dad will ground me for sure." She sighed dramatically. "Do you ever feel like your life is over?"

He tensed, unwillingly thinking about the accident years ago. *Did Belle tell her?* He doubted it. Before he could formulate an answer, the teen chatterbox went on.

"I do. And it's not even fair, because I didn't mean for it to happen. It just looked wrong, you know?" He recovered again and cleared his throat.

"Wrong time, wrong place?" he suggested.

"Yeah!" she said excitedly. "Dad is going to be mad. And Belle will lecture me, I'm sure. Which means I'll hear it twice, because Mike will mimic her . . . " she chattered on.

Eric's mind wandered a moment. *Is this what Belle meant? Was it just bad luck? No, it had to have been more.* He felt bitterness creep back into him. *God knew what He was doing.* At the same time, part of him didn't fully believe that either. He heard Kelli, still rambling, and tuned back into what she was saying.

" . . . something about being more responsible and not procrastinating, which I wasn't, but come on. She'll probably tell me some other deep thing, like . . . "

"Grow from it?" He could practically hear Belle saying it herself.

"Yeah! Exactly."

He smiled. Somewhere in the back of his mind, it registered that Kelli was all right.

"Mom wouldn't have lectured me," she said sadly.

That surprised Eric. He certainly didn't open up easily,

and here Kelli was dropping a potential emotional bombshell in his lap. Cautiously, he asked:

"Do you think about her a lot?"

She shrugged. "I guess. She would be more understanding about this."

"Belle will be understanding too, I imagine," he said, trying to help.

Kelli considered it for a minute.

"Maybe. I think she over-does it, you know? Trying to make up for Mom. Don't get me wrong, I'm glad Belle's around. It would have been way bad if she hadn't come back."

"Come back?"

"She was in California, at school," Kelli said. "When Mom died, she moved back here."

Eric was impressed. The more he learned about Belle, the more he admired her. She never seemed to give up or let anything get her down. And she seemed to put the needs of others before her own. They sat in silence a minute more and then Eric nudged her shoulder with his own.

"Time to go," he said, getting up. Reluctantly Kelli followed him to his car.

The ride to the Watson home was blissfully quiet as Kelli seemed to have run out of things to say. Eric pulled the car in front of the house and waited for Kelli to get out.

"Any ideas on how I can get out of this?" she asked.

"Be honest?" he suggested. Kelli groaned.

"I'm toast." With that, she got out of the car. "Thanks, Mr. Landry." The door shut, and Eric watched until she safely made it inside the house.

Eric had to smile at the teenage drama. Even though his head was still spinning from some of her chattering, he hoped she would "survive" this challenge and not get punished too harshly.

As he walked in from his garage, he called out to Mrs. Haygood. When he got no answer, he continued on through the kitchen and went to his bedroom. *She must be out at the store.*

He tossed his coat and tie on a lounge in the sitting area and kept going until he reached the bed. His eyes wandered to the picture of himself and his wife in happier times. He picked it up. It hurt that she wasn't there. It was still so raw sometimes, even though he knew he could do nothing about it. Perhaps it was just nostalgia, wishing for something long gone. On the other hand, he couldn't feel too angry about it anymore.

Something had changed.

Eric put the picture back in its place and began digging through the top drawer of the nightstand. His wife's things were still there, novels, papers, and a journal. He kept digging until he found a set of leather-bound scriptures. He pulled them out and looked at the cover. It was engraved with his wife's name: Sarah Landry. Eric ran his fingers over the lettering. With a deep breath, he sat back against the headboard, and opened the scriptures and began reading.

Belle came home a couple of hours after Kelli had been dropped off. Dinner was frozen pizza, so the cleanup was fast. Everyone sat in the living room afterwards. Kelli was quietly doing homework for a change and Mike was playing a video game. After a test, Belle liked to unwind doing something fun. She sat playing chess with her father.

"How did your exam go today?" he asked, moving a pawn.

Kelli immediately looked up, guilt written all over her face. Belle shot her a knowing grin.

"I was asking Belle," Watson clarified.

Kelli relaxed and returned to her reading.

"It was fine. I probably could have done better, but I'm happy with it," Belle said.

"You're almost done," he noted proudly.

"Just two more classes."

"Does that mean you'll have those initials after your name?" Mike piped up. He leaned to the left in front of the video game, as if his body movement affected where his virtual player went.

"If I really wanted to," Belle answered, "but it's not a huge deal. Most people don't do that."

"But it'd be cool. It's like you're a surgeon," he said excitedly.

"Except with no ability to operate," she corrected him.

Mike shrugged. "At least you'd have a cool car."

Kelli perked up at the mention of a car.

"You know who has a cool car? Mr. Landry!" she said, reverting to her usual chattering speed.

Watson glanced at his younger daughter disapprovingly. Kelli slouched back in front of her homework.

"What?" she mumbled. "I'm already grounded; can't I talk?" Belle nearly laughed, but she didn't want Kelli to take it as teasing.

They continued their respective activities in silence for a minute more and then Belle took her father's knight.

"It was nice of him to pick her up," Belle commented. Her mind had been running all day about that, and though it caught her off-guard, she was thrilled that Eric would be so thoughtful and kind.

"The least he could do when he has you slaving away," her father grunted.

"Dad," Belle warned.

Both Mike and Kelli had stopped what they were doing to listen.

"All the more reason it was nice of him," she said. Belle moved her bishop and took her father's queen. "Check!" she exclaimed.

Chapter Ten

$\mathcal{E}$ric bowed towards the wall in his exercise room and then launched into a martial arts routine. His arms and legs moved with precise control. He launched into a series of twists and kicks. He turned and did a roundhouse kick near the door.

His heart almost stopped when he saw Belle standing there, inches away from his extended leg. Quickly, he retracted out of the kick, while Belle jumped back, gasping.

"Eric!"

"Sorry!" he quickly apologized. "Are you okay? I didn't hit you, did I?" Belle shook her head.

"No, I'm fine. Um, I mean, I can . . . I'll tell you later," she said, turning to leave.

"No, uh, it's all right." He stepped back, his eyes on the floor until he felt like he wasn't blushing.

"Thank you, for taking care of Kelli. It was really sweet of you to do that," Belle blurted out.

"It was no trouble," he replied nonchalantly.

Belle smiled, her awkwardness fading.

"Well, thank you anyway. I'll get your email pulled up. Kyle Kincaid should have sent your itinerary by now."

He nodded and let out a sigh as Belle left. Eric returned to the starting position of his routine and smiled.

~~~~

Later when they broke for lunch, Belle was surprised to see bags of fast food from the local burger joint sitting on the ornate dining table. Belle sat across from Eric, and began eating her fries.

"I didn't think you liked fast food," she said between fries.

"Why wouldn't I?" he asked.

"I've just never seen you eat it."

Eric smiled.

"You don't know everything about me," he teased and then took a big bite out of the burger.

Belle smiled and continued to eat her lunch. Eric watched her for a moment and then put down his burger.

"May I ask you something?" he asked anxiously.

Belle shrugged. "Sure."

"Did . . . when your mother died, how did you . . . " he struggled trying to find the right word, ". . . react?"

Belle sensed he was being really serious about this.

"Like anyone else, I guess," she said. "We were devastated. And I missed her so much. I still do. But I knew things would be all right."

Eric frowned. "How?" he asked.

"What do you mean?"

"How did you know that God wasn't just putting you through some trial, testing you?" he asked earnestly.

"Maybe He was. But I won't fault Him for it. He knows what I can handle better than I do. Besides, it's not like I went through it alone," she said, glancing upward. "It happened. I trusted God, and He helped me through it. It wasn't easy; it took time to heal, but He was there for me every step of the way."

Eric sat back in his chair, digesting her words.

"You're stronger than I am," he finally said.

"I don't know about that. I mean, you gave up drinking."

"I *started* drinking," he countered.

"But not everyone can get over it. You did," she said with admiration.

Eric ducked his head bashfully. It meant a lot to him to hear her say that and to know she meant it. He tried to shrug it off and then he looked up and caught her eye.

"It's amazing what you can get through with the right help," Belle said with a smile.

Belle looked down at her meal and picked up the burger, missing Eric's gaze as he studied her admiringly.

Later that afternoon, Eric began packing his briefcase with the documents he would need for his business trip. Belle handed him a folder and watched as he stowed it in his briefcase.

The printer came to life and Belle grabbed the page it printed.

"Boarding pass," she said, handing it to Eric.

"Thanks," he said, placing it in the inside pocket of the briefcase.

"So how long will you be gone?" she asked.

"Depends. Three or four days, maybe."

Eric straightened up, and he and Belle silently regarded each other. The moment felt awkward to both of them. They had become close and the moment felt oddly domestic, but their arrangement was anything but. Even so, neither could suppress a semi-goofy smile.

"Um, well, have a good trip," Belle said.

"Thanks," he said and then took a step toward her as if to hug her goodbye. Eric stopped and quickly diverted to pull something off the bookshelf.

"See you when you get back," she said.

Eric nodded. "See you." She left for her other job, and Eric watched as she drove off down the driveway. He glanced at the clock, wondering how long he could survive without seeing Belle.

While Eric was gone, Belle continued her regular duties. She made sure things didn't get behind at the Landry Mansion and managed to keep up her studies and work at the orthodontics office. Eric had been gone for a couple of days when Belle sat at the reception desk, preparing an appointment list for the following day.

"So, he's been gone?" Anna stated more than asked as she came up behind her.

"Yeah," Belle nodded. "He comes back in two days."

She continued focusing on her work while Anna stood there expectantly.

"So . . . do you miss him?" Anna prodded.

Belle said nothing and kept working. She wasn't ready to answer that kind of question, not to Anna or even herself.

"We should make the most of it. Go do something fun," Anna persisted.

"Um, yeah," Belle stammered, coming out of her thoughts.

"I know Craig's been asking about you, if you're still open to that."

"Craig," Belle groaned.

"What?"

"Last time I saw him, I was kind of rude. Well, not really, but still . . . " Her voice drifted off.

"Yeah, he told me about that."

"What'd he say?"

"I wouldn't worry. He just wants to see you," Anna said.

Belle sighed and went back to work. She would worry about Craig another time. At that moment she didn't have the energy. Dr. Thompson called her right then, giving her a blessed excuse to think about other things.

Later, Belle sat preparing an instrument tray for the next appointment. She opened the sterilized packs of instruments and laid them on the paper towel covering the metal tray. Out of the corner of her eye, Belle saw movement in the waiting area. Thinking it was the next patient Belle walked out to greet him. Instead, to her dismay, Craig stood at the reception desk, chatting with his cousin. He turned when Belle walked out and gave her his standard charming smile.

"Hey Belle."

"Hi."

"I heard you have a few days off from the Rich and Richer," he said.

"Mostly," Belle said, forcing herself to smile despite the obvious jab at Eric. "I still have a few things to do, but . . . "

"Well, great!" he jumped in. "Want to go grab some lunch?"

Belle looked at Craig. She couldn't miss the hopeful gleam in his eyes. She didn't want to hurt him.

"Well, all right," she agreed.

He took her to a nice sit-down restaurant that specialized in steak and seafood. The food was great, the company tolerable, and the conversation . . . well . . .

"You have to admit, it's not easy putting up with that," he said with a laugh.

"No, it's not." Belle tried to smile along, but she was getting bored.

"So, how's your family?" Craig asked, taking a sip of his drink.

"Um, they're good," Belle said.

"Anna mentioned something about your sister."

She laughed. "Kelli's fine now. I'm not worried."

"It must be hard," he said.

"What?" she frowned.

"Well, I mean, you're kind of a surrogate mother for her. It must have been hard on you." Craig stared deeply into her eyes.

Belle was surprised at how personal the conversation became but decided she couldn't avoid it.

"It was an adjustment," she said mildly.

Craig leaned across the table and took Belle's hand in his. He scooted his chair a little closer, creating an uncomfortable intimacy for Belle.

"You're amazing. You'll make a great mother," he said, looking deeply into her eyes. He wasn't blinking, which was freaking Belle out.

She wanted to run as far away as possible. She couldn't understand where he got his nerve. She tried to smile for his benefit, but she was sure it came out more like a pained expression.

Belle tried to subtly withdraw her hand from his. When she had freed herself from the bear trap, she quickly grabbed her glass and took a long drink.

They continued the meal for an agonizing 45 minutes. The waiter came and cleared their plates and asked if they wanted any dessert. Belle thought if she had to stay there another minute, she was going to end up losing all sense of politeness. She eagerly turned down his offer of a single serving soufflé for two with the excuse that she needed to get back to work.

Craig paid the bill and drove her back to the orthodontics office. He walked her up to the office and stood at the reception desk while Belle put her purse away.

"I rented some movies, if you want come over tonight," he said smiling at her.

"Actually, I have some studying to do," she said politely.

Not to be deterred, Craig pressed on.

"All right. You free tomorrow night?"

Belle looked at him startled at his persistence. He chuckled and then explained.

"I just want to maximize my time with you, before Mr. Riches gets back."

Belle sighed. She was tired of people belittling Eric. *If only they would take the time to get to know him.* Of course, Eric didn't make it easy for her or anyone else to get close to him.

"Why do you always try to make fun of him?" she asked.

"Because," he shrugged, "everyone knows he's a difficult guy. It's why they call him the Beast."

Belle looked down sadly. She realized it was useless to try to convince Craig otherwise.

"Thanks for lunch. I've got to get back to work." Belle turned to work on patient files, but Craig stopped her again.

"Look, Belle, if I seem out of line, it's only because I know how great you are."

"Craig—"

"I just want you to get everything you deserve," he said, "and more. You're special that way." He kept looking into her eyes, as if to hypnotize her into agreement. Finally, he turned and left.

Anna came up behind her, having heard everything.

"So, how do you like Craig now?" she teased.

Belle tried not to shudder and turned to her work.

Eric climbed gratefully into the cab. The day had been

grueling with one marathon meeting running into another. He was glad to be going back to his hotel and wanted nothing more than sleep. Well, almost nothing more. He missed Belle. It bothered him, but not enough to stop him from pulling out his cell phone.

He began to dial her number and then stopped. *I need a reason to call.* He decided he could call about how things were at his office, or something. *I can wing it.* Eric dialed her number again and waited while the phone rang.

"Hello?" she answered.

"Hi," he said.

"Eric?"

He froze for a second. *This isn't going to work.*

"Uh," he struggled, "I'm on my way back to the hotel and just wanted to check in. See how things are going."

He winced and held his breath, waiting to see if she bought it.

"Everything's fine. It's quiet, but . . . " she replied. She sounded a little tired. Oddly, Eric himself felt invigorated now just talking with her. *It's because you're trying to figure out what to say next.*

"Yeah," he said. *Brilliant reply. Quickly, something else to say!* "Um, how are your classes?" He nearly groaned. *That's the best I can come up with?*

"Good. I was just finishing an assignment," Belle said.

Eric grimaced. "Oh, sorry, I didn't mean to interrupt."

"No, no. It's okay."

And then silence. *Your turn, Eric.* But his mind went blank. *What else do I say?*

"Okay. Well, um, give me a call if you need anything," he finally said.

"I will. Thanks."

"See you when I get back?" Eric held his breath.

"Okay," she said. He could picture her smiling, which was a good thing. "Good night."

"Bye." He hung up, and quickly tried to catch his breath. He could have done worse, but not much. Resisting the urge to bang his head against the cab window, Eric made himself settle back into the seat.

Belle flopped back on her bed and relished the moment. *He called.* She was surprised, to say the least, but in a good way. *Not like when Craig calls or comes by.*

She sighed. *Homework, Belle.* She had to focus on that. And she tried to, but her mind kept wandering back to Eric. After five minutes of fighting it, Belle gave up.

She went to the mansion. She walked into the dark office, finding his desk lamp by memory. She turned the light on and sat behind Eric's desk. Her textbook in hand, Belle looked around the room for a moment and then settled down to read. Maybe being here would help her study. But she couldn't seem to focus for long and found herself gazing around the office again. Her eyes settled on the framed flask. Setting the textbook aside, Belle rose and went to inspect the flask closer. She picked up the wooden frame and felt the weight of the half-full bottle inside. She ran her fingers over the corners and then turned it over. Something was written on the back of the frame.

'NEVER AGAIN,' it read. She smiled and returned the flask to its place on the shelf.

Belle looked at the desk where her textbook lay, but instead of returning to read it, she walked out of the office. She wandered through the mansion, stopping to look in all the rooms. Each seemed to reflect Eric in some way. She stopped in the sitting room and examined a portrait of Eric that hung on the wall. She'd never noticed it before. The artist seemed to have captured the real Eric, both his softer and more mysterious, brooding sides. She smiled and looked away.

Chapter Eleven

Anna sat at the reception desk, updating patient files. She smiled when the door opened and in walked her cousin.

"Craig!" she said with a sly smile. "How was the date?"

His face fell despite his attempts to force a smile.

"All right." He couldn't hide the disappointment in his tone either.

"Just all right? I thought you'd have so much fun."

"I did," he explained quickly. "I mean I know she's amazing, and I know she's the one, you know, who can stand by me in all I'm supposed to do in life . . . "

Anna stopped what she was doing. "What?"

But Craig paid no attention to Anna's reaction and continued on.

"But Belle . . . Why's she working for this Landry guy? I can never spend time with her because she's always at his beck-and-call."

"Um, well, she kind of has to be," Anna explained.

"What do you mean?"

Anna took a deep breath. "Belle's dad was working at Landry's mansion, and broke something. Landry said he was going to have him fired if he didn't pay for it, or something like that. So Belle's working for Landry until it's all good."

Craig's face darkened. "Sounds like extortion."

Anna shrugged. "It's messed up," she said, "but at least

Belle's dad still has his job. That's all that matters."

Anna went back to her work. Craig lingered a moment, lost in thought and then left abruptly.

Eric pulled into the garage. He was so glad to be home. He popped the trunk and gathered his luggage and headed into the house. He found Mrs. Haygood making another one of her pies in the kitchen. He paused to greet her.

"Mrs. Haygood."

"Hello, Eric," she said, looking up from the fruit filling. "How was your trip?"

"Good. I'm glad I'm back though." Oddly enough, it was true. He couldn't remember when he'd been more pleased to be home.

"I'll be right in to unpack those," Mrs. Haygood said as he walked passed.

"Thank you," he called over his shoulder and then made his way to his bedroom.

He dropped his bags on the bed and took off his coat and tie, placing them on a lounger. He continued on to the master bathroom and began to freshen up. He was washing his face when Mrs. Haygood came in a moment later. She unzipped the bags and began putting the clothes in their proper places.

"Have you seen Belle lately?" Eric asked as he dried his face with a hand towel.

"Yes. She's checked in every day."

"Really?"

Mrs. Haygood dug deeper into the bag and was surprised to pull out a set of scriptures. She recognized the set—it had belonged to Sarah. She placed them on the nightstand with a pleased smile.

"Mmmm hmm. She's a good one," she said. She pulled

out Eric's shaving kit next.

"She is," he agreed. He saw the kit in her hand and took it from her. He began to put away everything, his toothbrush, razor and so forth. Mrs. Haygood was surprised at that, since he normally just let her do everything.

She put on her motherly smile. "When are you going to let her off the hook? I'd say Belle's done more than enough time."

Eric sighed. "I know."

"You could give her the choice to stay, if you want her to," Mrs. Haygood suggested.

"Yeah. I'm just not sure she'd take it." He ran his fingers through his hair.

"You might be surprised, Eric," she said as she left the room. Eric looked after her, wondering if she was right.

Craig walked up to Belle's door. He took a deep breath, checked his appearance in the window and then rang the bell. A few moments later, Belle came to the door.

"Craig," she said.

"I know you might be busy, but I was wondering if you wanted to go out tonight. Or tomorrow. Whenever," he asked, the charming grin shining away.

"Oh. I . . ." she stammered. It took her a moment, but she knew she had to end this. "Craig, I'd rather not."

Belle looked down. She felt bad for what she was about to do, but subtlety hadn't worked.

"I don't want to lead you on," she explained. "I'm not interested in you like that. If you don't mind, I'd rather keep our friendship, but nothing more."

Craig stumbled back off the porch in surprise. He blinked several times, like he was processing what she'd said.

"Belle, come on. I know you have a lot on your mind, but I'm willing to wait. I know this is right."

Belle took an awkward breath.

"The reason isn't my schedule," she tried again.

Craig was stunned, but managed to nod his understanding.

"Well, I'll . . . " He retreated a few steps. "When you change your mind, I'll be here."

"Craig, I'm not going—" she started to say. Craig stopped her with the raise of his hand, his fingers hovering in front of her lips. Belle nearly jumped back.

And then, he turned and got into his car. Belle sighed and went back into the house.

Craig drove away angrily. He pulled out his phone and dialed a number.

"Peterson Repair," the call was answered.

"Yeah, this is Eric Landry," Craig said. "I'd like to lodge a complaint." He would make it easier for Belle to see that he was the one for her.

Eric paced around his office, tossing his cell phone back and forth between his hands. He stopped, took a deep breath, and dialed Belle's number.

"Hello?" Belle answered.

"Belle," Eric said, almost in relief.

"Hey, how was your trip?" He could hear the smile in her voice.

"Ah, good," he answered. "Listen, I'll tell you all about it, but I was wondering if you could come over," he said, a trace of nerves in his voice.

"Oh, sure. There's probably a lot to do."

"No, it's not that. I just . . . I wanted to talk to you about something."

"Okay," she answered, and Eric noted she sounded a little nervous. That of course only increased his anxiety, but he held it in check. "Give me a half hour, and I'll be right there."

"Okay." Eric said goodbye and hung up. He grinned like a teenage boy who just successfully asked out a girl, and for some reason, he was all right with that.

Belle stood in front of the living room mirror, checking her appearance. She had just changed her clothes and now adjusted her blouse and checked her hair. *It's not a date! You're just going to work.*

But that didn't curb her eagerness to see Eric. She had missed him, and it sounded like he might have missed her too. *Don't think that. You may just be disappointed*, she thought.

Belle caught her dad's reflection in the mirror. Not knowing he was home already, she turned to face him.

"Dad?" she called out.

Watson lowered himself into his lounge chair. He looked defeated and Belle could see tears in his eyes. Stunned, she went to his side.

"That horrible . . . " he began.

"Dad, what happened?" she asked as she knelt beside him.

"They fired me."

Belle's heart skipped a beat. "What? Why?"

He looked at his daughter sadly.

"They got a call," he said with a shuddering breath, "from Eric Landry."

A sharp pain pierced her mind and heart. Belle rose and sat down on the sofa, stunned. It didn't make sense. *He wouldn't do this.*

Would he?

Suddenly, anger rushed through her. Anger at Eric,

certainly, but also at herself. She couldn't believe she'd been taken in by his act. She grabbed her keys and left.

As she drove to the Landry mansion, the idea of Eric going back on their deal festered. For him to betray her—it was the ultimate disappointment.

Or maybe, it was that she had fallen for him, for someone who could be so cruel. Tears coursed down her face as she replayed all her time with him through her mind.

Eric stood in front of his bedroom mirror and buttoned up a lavender dress shirt. He tried it with the top button done and then undone and couldn't decide which he liked better. He sighed in frustration and walked to the closet, unbuttoning his shirt as he went. He pulled out a deep blue shirt and buttoned it in front of the mirror. He fingered through his hair as butterflies danced in his stomach. He sighed again.

"This is ridiculous," he said to himself.

The sound of the door opening and closing kicked the butterflies up another notch. Eric gave the mirror and his hair one last look and then went to meet Belle.

He smiled and walked down the hallway. Belle met him in the great room. She stepped into the light and he was surprised to see her face stained with tears.

"Belle?"

Belle stared at him incredulously. She swiftly crossed the distance between them in three big steps and slapped him across the face. Eric stepped back, shocked.

"How . . . how could you?" she said through new tears.

He looked at her, confused.

"After all this time. I thought you were different, that what everyone said about you wasn't true." She choked back a sob. "I even *defended* you."

Eric couldn't make sense of her words. "Belle . . . " he stammered.

"Don't! I fell for it once, this act. I won't anymore."

Belle stepped back.

"You really are a beast," she said. Eric looked after her a moment, the hurt and confusion warring inside him. Before he could try to say anything, she ran out the door.

"Belle! Wait!" he called out. He followed her, but she didn't stop or look back.

What happened? Eric thought. Everything was going so well, but now he wasn't sure what to do, or worse, what he might have done to upset her.

Chapter Twelve

$\mathcal{B}$elle closed her bedroom door behind her and leaned against it. As the full impact of what had happened hit her, she slid down to the floor. Tears slid down her face, dropping onto her knees.

After a few minutes, she dried her eyes and climbed onto her bed. She lay on her back and wondered how she could be so foolish. There was a reason everyone called Eric the Beast, but she let her heart look past that, only to be deceived.

Her phone rang and she reached for it on her nightstand. She glanced at the caller ID. 'Eric Landry,' it read. She hit the button to silence the ring and tossed the phone on the floor.

Eric let the phone ring a few more times and then gave up. He decided he'd try again the next morning. Over the next few days, he tried repeatedly to call Belle. His calls went unanswered.

He decided to try another route. He paced around his office and dialed her home number. His pacing increased as he waited for someone to answer.

"Hello?" It was Kelli.

"Kelli? Is Belle there?" he asked, thinking he had an ally in the teen.

Kelli hesitated and then asked, "Who is this?"

"It's Eric Landry." He heard the long silence his name effected.

"I don't think anyone here wants to talk to you," she said. Eric waited, hoping she wouldn't hang up on him. "Sorry." It was an afterthought, and even though Kelli hung up at that point, Eric appreciated the little bit of understanding.

He shut his cell phone. Frustrated, he raked his hands through his hair and continued pacing. He didn't know what was wrong, and it made it even harder to figure out how he could fix things.

Belle worked diligently to refill bracket containers at the orthodontics office. Anna watched her with concern. She had not been herself for days.

"Are you all right?" Anna asked cautiously.

"Fine."

"No, you're not," she said. She knew when her friend was lying. "Look, it's terrible what Landry did, but—"

Belle ignored her and moved away to work on another task. Anna sighed.

Belle had no interest in talking about Eric Landry. He had continued to call her and she had adopted a strict ignore-all-calls policy when his number flashed on the ID window. She wasn't going to be caught up in his cruel ways again.

Eric was beyond puzzled. He kept going over everything in his mind and still came up blank as to what he had done wrong. He tried to distract himself by shooting baskets, but it was useless. He couldn't focus and after missing three shots in a row, he gave up and began pacing the court. He decided this craziness had to end and if he had to see her in person to make her listen, he would.

Eric pulled up to the Watson home. A brief flash of memory went through his mind of the last time he was there with Belle. He went to the door and knocked. The curtains were closed, so he couldn't see if anyone was at home.

Luckily, someone answered the door. But Eric winced when he saw it was Mr. Watson. The two men stared at each in silence for an awkward moment. Belle's father appeared to be quite upset upon seeing him there.

"Mr. Landry," he said firmly. Eric didn't often feel intimidated, but given the circumstances, he was more than uncomfortable.

"Is Belle here?" he managed to ask.

"No," Watson said, and he went to shut the door. Eric stuck his hand out, halting the door's progress.

"Wait, please," he pled. "I just need to talk to her. Could you ask her to call me?"

"You have a lot of nerve, Mr. Landry," Watson said, his voice firm. "Maybe you think you can get away with anything, but you won't hurt my family anymore. Go away. I'm busy looking for a job." He slammed the door and Eric took a step back.

He drove home and went directly to his office. He sat behind his desk, trying to make sense of Watson's words. He began to piece it together. 'I'm busy looking for a job,' he had said. *He'd been fired?*

Frowning, Eric looked through the papers on his desk until he found the one he wanted. He dialed the office phone and waited.

"Peterson Repair," a person answered.

"Yes, this is Eric Landry," he said.

"Is something wrong, sir?"

"No, everything is fine here," Eric said, "but . . . is a

Mr. Watson still working for you?"

"No, sir, we fired him just like you asked us when you called."

Eric blinked.

"Fired? But that wasn't me that called. There must be some kind of misunderstanding," he said. He sighed, rubbing his head and the ache that was starting to pound there. *How did they think I called?*

"Look," he said, "I would really appreciate it if you could give him his job back."

Belle walked in the door, thoroughly exhausted after a long day of work and classes. Her family was washing the dinner dishes.

"Hi," Belle said, sitting down to eat the plate of food they had left for her.

"Guess what?" Kelli said excitedly.

She looked at her younger sister with a raised brow. "What?"

Mike piped up. "Dad got his job back!"

"Really?" Belle didn't expect that.

Her father nodded as he scrubbed the roasting pan. She noticed the smile on his face.

"Guess the guilt got to him," he said, placing the pan to drain.

Belle wasn't sure what to think. Of course, she was relieved about her dad having his job again, but . . . She sighed and dug into her meal in earnest.

"He called again," Kelli announced in a sing-song voice. She handed Belle the message. Without looking at it, Belle crumbled the message up and tossed it away. She resumed her meal, while Kelli sighed and went back to the dishes.

Later Watson found Belle watching TV in the living room. He smiled. She had had very little time to relax, and it was good to see her taking it a bit easier now.

"Taking a break?" he asked sitting in his chair.

Belle smiled and turned the TV off.

"Yeah. I'm tired of catching up on everything—school, laundry, sleep," she said. She stretched and leaned back into the couch cushions.

"Want some dessert? Kelli tried her hand at instant pudding."

"No, I'm okay," she declined with a smile.

"It can't be too bad," Watson argued on Kelli's behalf. "I mean, how can anyone mess up instant pudding."

"Believe me, Dad, Kelli can find a way."

They shared a laugh. Watson quieted and glanced at his daughter.

"You know," he started, "I'm almost glad I was fired for awhile."

"Really?"

Watson nodded.

"You didn't have to put up with all the Landry hassle anymore."

"Oh. Well, that was more his doing than mine, but I was happy to do it anyway," she said, shrugging.

Watson tilted his head to the side.

"You gave up a lot. Just like when your mother died."

"Dad, it really wasn't a big deal."

He dismissed her modesty with a shake of his head.

"I've always been proud of you," he said. "But I want you to start looking out for yourself now."

Belle frowned. "Dad, I was happy to come—"

"No, I know. But you've more than earned the right to a little happiness."

Belle smiled.

"Find it, whatever makes you happy," he said. "For you."

He smiled at her and patted her knee as he rose and left. Belle watched him go back to his bedroom and thought about what he had said.

The next day, Belle walked across campus to her next class. Her cell phone rang as she crossed the quad. She stopped and dug it out of her purse. She sighed when she saw who the caller was. *Time to end this*, she thought. She needed to put this behind her. She pushed the answer button.

"Please stop calling," she said quickly.

"Belle, wait—" Eric pled with her.

"Thank you for getting my dad's job back, but I've had enough."

"No, Belle, it was a mistake—" he tried to explain.

"Yes, it was," she shot back. She made herself calm down. She didn't want to drag this out any longer than necessary. "You never should have held my dad's job over his head in the first place."

Belle hung up on him before he could think of anything to say to that. *'You never should have held my dad's job over his head in the first place.'* Eric leaned his arms on his desk.

Resting his head in his hands, he ran through everything again in his mind. She was right, of course. Guilt dampened his mood even more.

He looked up and stared off into nothing. Finally his gaze rested on the framed flask. He considered it a moment and then looked away. He didn't want his thoughts to go down that path. He left the office for another walk around his grounds.

~~~~

Belle gathered the used instruments from the treatment station and began cleaning up the area. She sprayed some disinfectant on a rag and began wiping the chair down.

"You working later?" Anna asked, coming up behind her.

"What do you mean?" Belle was working through the end of the day, and Anna knew that.

"At Landry's."

Belle felt her heart clench at the mention of Eric.

"No," she said resolutely.

"Oh," Anna said. "Have you talked to him since . . . "

"Yeah."

"So you're still ticked."

Belle stopped her work. "Wouldn't you be?"

"Yeah, but . . . he tried to make it up to you."

"He went back on our deal," Belle said. "Just because his sliver of a conscience got through, doesn't mean I'm doing anything for him."

Anna smiled.

"Well, at least you'll have more time for Craig."

She snickered as she saw Belle tense up at the mention of her cousin.

"I'm kidding. He told me about the other day."

Belle relaxed. "You're cruel," she said with a laugh. "You're okay with it?"

"Sure!" Anna said. "He may be my cousin, but I know how he can be."

Later in the day after the last patient left, Anna was going over the patient schedules for the next day. Belle wiped down the last of the treatment chairs and was closing down the rest of the office. The bell above the door sounded, causing both women to look up. It was Craig.

He waved to Anna and walked over to Belle.

"Hi," he said. "How have you been?"

"Fine, thanks," Belle said, smiling tightly.

"I heard what happened," he said sympathetically. "I'm sorry about your dad, and his job." Belle froze for a second. *How does he know?* She glanced across the office to Anna, and sighed.

"I'm more sorry any of it happened," she said.

"Listen, if you want to go out, get your mind off things, I'm here."

Belle smiled and looked down at the ground.

"Thanks, but I'll manage," she said. She turned away to tidy up another area, and realized she was holding her breath until she heard Craig leave.

She sighed, and with a smile, shook her head.

Chapter Thirteen

Meanwhile, Eric wasn't faring well. He had trouble sleeping and work was just a chore for him, something he'd never felt before. Mrs. Haygood grew more concerned as the days passed. She noticed the bags and dark shadows under his eyes. He hadn't been eating much either. And on more than one occasion she had caught him casting frequent glances at his flask.

One night, Eric lay in his bed, completely awake. He had tossed and turned, hit his pillow to plump it, all to no avail. Finally he gave up all pretense of sleep and went for a walk on the grounds. He went outside in the cold wearing nothing but thin sweat pants and a dark t-shirt. He walked along the path he had taken Belle on that one day. Never had he felt quite so alone. The cold air had no effect on him as he continued his trek. An hour later he went back into the house and fell into a fitful sleep.

The next day Eric got dressed, although he looked like a shadow of his usual polished self. He went to the office without breakfast and tried to work for awhile. He felt restless and couldn't concentrate on anything.

Mrs. Haygood was preparing lunch in the kitchen when he walked by, evidently giving up on work for now.

"Eric?" she called to him. "Lunch will be just a minute."

"Thanks, but I'm not hungry," he said flatly and kept on walking.

Mrs. Haygood bit her lip in concern. In all the years she had worked for him, she'd never seen him so broken.

After another failed attempt to sleep, Eric got up and paced restlessly. He ached from the inside out. He began to breathe heavily as he felt the weight of his agony. But he didn't know what to do to escape its oppressive grip.

He walked to the sitting room and sat on Belle's bench. The warped Book of Mormon lay on a nearby sofa. He stared at it. Part of him felt like all this was God's way of testing him. Part of him hated being tested, and he wanted to throw the book away.

But he knew he couldn't. His body shook with the conflicting emotions inside. *Why can't I just work this out? What do I have to do?*

And suddenly he knew. He was a solitary man by nature, but he couldn't do this alone. Years ago, he had tried that and failed miserably.

With no other solution and nowhere else to turn, he fell to his knees in front of the sofa. He began to pray. Tears coursed down his face as he tried to pour out his heart.

Eric opened his eyes and saw the book again. He rose to his feet and grabbed it.

He knew what he would do.

Eric walked determinedly down the hall to his office and went straight to where the flask sat. He picked it up with shaking hands. The amber liquid inside sloshed a little with the movement and he felt its pull. The weakness angered and saddened him at the same time.

Staring at the frame, he broke the glass and grabbed the offending bottle. The broken frame and shards of glass fell to the floor.

He stepped over the mess and walked out with the flask in hand.

Anna and Belle sat in a booth at a nearby café. It was Saturday morning and their day off.

"I'm starving. I hear their muffins are great," Anna said, rubbing her hands together in anticipation.

"That might be good," Belle conceded as she looked at her menu. "Why am I here again?" She knew Anna had set something up with Craig.

"To eat?" Anna suggested innocently.

Belle saw through that and shot her friend a look. Anna laughed.

"Look, Craig begged me. He just wanted to see you one more time, and he swore if you still felt . . . whatever, he'd back off."

Belle sighed. "At least it's breakfast. I always skip it, and by 10 o'clock, I'm dying."

"It'll be worth it, to your stomach at least."

"Where is he anyway?" Belle said as she checked her watch.

"He called in a panic—turned his alarm off early," Anna explained. They spent a moment going over the menus.

"Hey," Belle said thoughtfully, "why did you tell Craig about my dad? I kind of wished he didn't know what happened, with the job, getting fired and everything . . . "

Anna frowned.

"But I didn't tell him."

"Really?"

"I told him about the whole you-working-for-Eric deal, but not about your dad getting fired. I figured he might rub it in, and that's the last thing you need."

Before Belle could weigh Anna's words any further, Craig walked in and slid next to her in the booth.

"Morning, girls," he said cheerfully.

"Hi Craig," Anna replied.

Belle tried to smile, but Anna's words were still bothering her as she turned them over and over in her mind.

"Craig," she started, "how did you know my dad got fired?"

He froze and then tried to shrug it off.

"Anna told me."

"No, I didn't," she rebutted.

"Oh." He shrugged again and smiled. "I must have heard it somewhere."

Belle watched him. *Why is he nervous? He's acting . . . Guilty.*

As the pieces fell into place, her smile fell. *He wouldn't. Would he?*

"Craig?" The suspicion was too strong to hide from her voice.

"Really," he said, swallowing anxiously. He looked back and forth to each girl, as if his wide-eye contact would help them believe his story. Their twin glares said it wasn't working.

"Did you call my dad's boss?" Belle couldn't stifle the accusation.

Craig turned to his cousin for help and she glared back, just as upset.

"No. Why would I?"

"Craig!" Anna gasped.

"I'm such an idiot," Belle said, her head sinking into her hands. She looked up and glared angrily at Craig. He leaned back from her in the booth.

"How *could* you?" she said.

"Belle," he tried, oozing charm, "the guy's awful. You

shouldn't—" That nailed it for Belle. She suddenly started pushing him away, disgusted but at the same time trying to get by him.

"I can't believe you!" her voice rose.

"Belle!" he pleaded.

She pushed him harder until he fell out of the booth and landed on the floor with a resounding thud on his backside. Belle grabbed her purse and quickly stepped over him.

Anna watched her friend leave and then turned back to her cousin. He still sat on the floor. She rolled her eyes.

"What?" he protested.

"You're such a loser."

Belle raced over to the Landry mansion. She slammed her car into park and got out, immediately breaking into a run towards the house.

"Eric?" she called out inside, desperate to find him.

She got no answer and so began systematically checking the house. She went into the master bedroom. The bed was unmade and his pajamas lay sprawled on the bedspread.

She ran through the kitchen and checked the spa room. She called out his name and was only greeted by the echo of her voice.

"Belle?" Mrs. Haygood called out from somewhere.

Belle turned around from the spa to see Mrs. Haygood walk in.

"Where's Eric?" she asked.

"I haven't seen him yet this morning," Mrs. Haygood replied.

Belle ran past her to the office. She glanced in quickly and then stopped when she caught site of broken glass. It was the flask, or rather the frame. The shards glinted up at her.

"He didn't . . . " she said to herself. *Could he have? Did he start drinking again?*

Mrs. Haygood came in behind her and saw the mess. A gasp escaped her lips.

"I'll call his cell phone," she said, quickly recognizing the danger Eric could be in. Belle watched as the housekeeper ran out of the room, picked up a phone and dialed. Belle turned to the mess and carefully picked up what was left of the frame. She gently turned it over and the inscription glared accusingly at her. 'NEVER AGAIN.'

Suddenly a cell phone rang. Belle looked in the direction of the ring and noticed Eric's cell phone dancing on the desk.

Mrs. Haygood came back in, the cordless phone in hand. Her shoulders slumped when she saw the cell phone. She hung up.

"Where would he go?" Belle asked.

"I don't know," Mrs. Haygood said. "I'll check the grounds."

Mrs. Haygood dashed out of the room to begin her search. But Belle didn't move. She looked around Eric's office, thinking. A picture on his desk caught her attention. She stood and picked it up, examining it more closely. *It's that place in the canyon, where we went after dinner.* That had to be where he went.

She dashed out the door and into her car. As she drove up the canyon, her eyes filled with tears. She was afraid of what he might have done or would do. She wiped the tears away and kept going. She had to find him and fast.

Twenty minutes later Belle pulled into the parking area by the lake. She breathed in relief when she saw Eric's car sitting there. She pulled her car to a stop next to his and got out. Belle scanned the lake for any sign of him. At first she saw nothing but frozen lake. Then on the far side of the lake she spotted a figure sitting on a fallen branch. Just seeing him flooded her with a measure of reassurance.

She ran around the lake towards him. She slowed as she got closer and approached him cautiously. He was dressed in jeans and a leather jacket, probably not warm enough out here, but he didn't seem to notice.

He stared unseeingly out over the icy lake. His eyes were red and he looked tired. Belle felt a spike of anger at Craig rise in her again and then dissipate.

Eric held the flask in his hands.

Belle watched as he unscrewed the cap and eyed it evenly. He stood up, still focused on the lake. She decided it was time to make her presence known, fearing if not he might take a drink.

"Eric," she said gently.

He turned, startled to hear her voice. He had thought he was alone and that he'd never hear her voice again. Belle walked to him slowly, her eyes on the flask in his hands.

"Belle." His heart sped up just seeing her here.

"What are you doing here?" she asked.

"Thinking."

"Just thinking?" Belle asked, nodding at the bottle.

Eric frowned and looked down at the flask. *Oh.* He understood how she might interpret this.

"Yeah."

Suddenly he drew his arm back and pitched the flask out into the lake. The bottle skidded and skipped across the ice until it finally sank through a hole in the lake's center. Belle watched the bottle and then turned back to Eric. Next to him on the log sat The Book of Mormon she had read at the mansion.

"What happened to the reminder?" she asked.

He shrugged. "I got tired of it hanging over my head."

She came closer to him.

"Why the change of mind?"

"It's overdue." Eric smiled, and after a moment, Belle did too.

"I'm sorry about your dad," he said with regret in his voice and face. He took a step toward her. "I never should have threatened him, or put you through all this."

"No, but . . . it wasn't all bad," she said.

"Really?" Eric blinked hopefully.

Belle nodded.

"Yeah. I got to know you, not the rumors. And I should have known better, that you wouldn't go back on everything. It was . . ." She paused, shaking her head. "It wasn't you."

"It sounds like me," he chuckled softly. "But . . . I don't want to be like that anymore. I've seen how you treat others, and how you've treated me, even when I was terrible to you."

He paused. "You make me want to be a better person."

Belle smiled and looked up at him.

"You sure it's me?" she asked.

"You played a part." He looked back to the lake, trying to sort out how he felt and how to explain it. "You helped me see what I tried to ignore. I realize now, after all this time, that I was never alone. I just wasn't listening."

Belle watched him and listened intently. She was amazed at the change in him, and more so that he was acknowledging it to himself too. He seemed at peace for the first time since she had met him.

"He does want me to be happy," Eric added. He smiled shyly.

"Does that mean you are happy?" she asked, teasing him a little. She stepped towards him.

"Getting there."

Belle stopped.

"It's not all perfect yet," Eric continued. "For example,

I don't have an assistant anymore. I was going to ask you to stay on."

Belle tried not to show her disappointment at that. She tried to smile.

"Oh. Yeah," she said, "I'll think about it. I still have school and my other job, but . . . "

Eric nodded. There was a faint smile tugging at his lips.

"Oh. Well, it was an excuse anyway," he said and looked away self-consciously.

"It's what?" she asked, caught a little off-guard.

Eric sighed and shifted around, struggling to find the right words.

"I've only cared about myself for so long. It's awkward now that I . . . care about someone else," he said. He tensed as he watched her digest his words.

Slowly, she smiled. Eric felt his heart lift. He pressed on:

"I just want to be with you. I don't deserve it, but I'll do whatever I can to try," he promised.

Amazingly, Belle didn't seem shocked like he thought she might be. A blush crept into her cheeks and she took another step towards him.

"You don't have to try too hard anymore. You make me happy," she said as she recalled her father's words.

Eric smiled and stepped towards her. Nothing was said as they looked at each other for a moment. A strand of her hair danced in the breeze. He reached out, unable to help himself, and tucked it behind her ear. He let his hand slide to her face and gently cupped her cheek, caressing it with his thumb. They smiled at each other, just inches apart. Eric couldn't resist any longer. He pulled her to him and kissed her tenderly.

It was a kiss that was the beginning of many more to come.

~~~~

With Eric's transformation and his renewed faith, the town discovered that the Beast was gone. In his stead was a kind, gentle man whose heart had been changed by the power of God, and the love of a woman named Belle.

And while their world wasn't perfect . . . they still lived happily ever after.

The End